D1028215

MY HUSBAND RAN OFF
WITH THE NANNY
AND GOD DO I MISS HER

by Tracy Davis

ISBN: 1-4392-1704-1
ISBN-13: 9781439217047

Visit www.booksurge.com to order additional copies.

*My Husband Ran Off With the Nanny
and God Do I Miss Her*

ONE

I pulled over obediently at the first flash and whirl, feeling that sickening pit-of-the-stomach dread, and emptied my purse on the front seat to try to find my driver's license. Let's see, the last time I saw it...I think it was in a coat pocket somewhere. I scrambled for my lipstick. "Please, dear God, please, don't let him arrest me. I'll go to church this very Sunday." I unrolled the window, attempting to look contrite and charming. "Merry Christmas, Officer! I am sooo sorry."

"License please?" he asked. He looked about twelve, so flirting was out.

"Well, that's the thing. It was stolen. I'm pretty sure. See?" I leaned back so he could see the contents of my purse while my fingers fluttered over them—chocolate-covered change, crumpled up TO DO lists from controlling husband Paul, a few broken cigarettes, a pair of sunglasses with one arm, a credit card, and Kleenex, but no driver's license.

The policeman was writing something on his pad. "You were pulled over for driving twenty-five miles over the speed limit in an HOV zone, switching lanes erratically, and displaying an inappropriate gesture to another vehicle." He wasn't acting friendly. "Road rage is a crime."

This wasn't looking good. My mother went to jail once for speeding, but that was in East Hampton and I was in D.C. Then I realized, to my absolute horror, that if he *did* arrest me, I would be dead because it was Friday and Monday was Christmas, which meant that no judge would consider working, which meant I would be in jail until Tuesday before I could even get out on bail! I could see it in the *Chevy Chase Gazette:* "Mrs. Carly Macalister, former mother of two, spent Christmas in the District of Columbia jail and, upon her return, her husband had understandably been granted an immediate divorce and full custody. Mrs. Macalister went mute from trauma and…"

I let out a wail and then started jabbering desperately at the cop. I think I was clinging to his collar. "Oh, Officer! I **know road rage is a crime and I hate those people who are so awful!** And I just have to tell you…" My eyes looked pleading and desperate, my voice was shaky, my whole body started going into minor convulsions, and I attempted a sniffle, "…I've *just* received tragic news! That's all. No road rage. Just a small reaction…to tragic news." I leaned toward him. "Someone I love is close to death!" (Me.) I grabbed a Kleenex, and there was my license underneath. "Here!" I shouted, startling him.

The officer waved his hand as if to say, 'Calm down, Lady,' and took my license. He stared at me, then the license, and then back at me, then back to the license—It took forever. Finally, he announced, "You're much prettier in person."

"Thank you, Officer." I was sobbing.

"Now, I want you to calm down. I'm going to give you a warning this time, okay?"

"Thank you, sir." Yes! Now, give me the license back and go away, I thought. But he studied it again.

"Catherine Russell Macalister. Chevy Chase." The officer thought for a moment. "You know, I remember pulling an elderly Catherine Russell over for speeding once. She was going ninety miles per hour. She must have been your mother. I can see the resemblance."

Oh no.

"I take after my father," I explained.

"Your mother was quite charming. Quite a woman." He smiled, remembering her, talking to himself.

'I'll give her my best,' I almost replied sarcastically. "Thank you, Officer, I'm just so upset right now." Damn my mother.

He handed me back my license. "Drive carefully."

"Yes, sir. I'll drive like a snail. Promise."

A very close call.

I let the officer pull out first and I sat there for a few minutes while I tried to stop shaking. I jabbed at the radio like it was a typewriter, searching for a Christmas carol, but all I could find were commercials and rap. "When are you going to play them, anyway?" I shouted at the radio, "New Years?" I was furious with my mother. She could have landed me in jail! She would have to slow down, no more sports cars for *her*—racing all over the place like a teenager. It was ridiculous.

Finally, I calmed down enough to creep back into the traffic.

Normally I would *never* attempt the nightmarish task of getting out of downtown Washington, D.C. during rush hour, but my real estate manager, Ellie, forced me to attend this idiotic seminar, three days before Christmas, called "*How to Make Simplicity and Patience the Cornerstones of Your Life.*" Apparently you learn this by sitting still for eight hours in a clammy basement classroom, interrupted only by a lunch hour spent shoving annoying people out of the way to cram in the purchase of as many gifts as possible for the children before returning to said increasingly claustrophobic basement. And, upon release from the basement, you tackle the very same stores to return everything purchased when in an irrational state of mind during lunch that, upon consideration, you realize are not items the kids will even like before attempting to get out of the city in the dark during rush hour when you are fussy, hungry, exhausted, and thirsty.

When my manager, Ellie, who normally adores me, called me into her office, I thought she was going to give me a present. It was the holidays, plus I was actually making money, and half of it went to her. I marched into her office with confidence.

"Carly, you're number two out of all the new real estate agents in the Washington, D.C., area. You could win 'Rookie of the Year.' It's that close." Ellie seemed baffled. Her eyebrows arched up into her black bangs.

"Right. So leave me alone," I answered cheerfully.

She ignored this and studied a paper in front of her. "You've sold seven houses in the last two months. That's incredible, considering I hardly see you work." She peered down at my briefcase, which I had emptied into my car before the meeting so she couldn't see my contracts, although they were more organized than my purse. "I thought we should go over your contracts. Where is all your paperwork?"

"Filed meticulously in my home office."

Her eyes narrowed. Then she sighed. "A customer of yours has complained that you race through yellow lights."

"I bet Maria Slovinski told you that. That rich, spoiled, whiney bitch complains about everything, Ellie."

"Carly, she's a *customer*."

I was getting antsy.

"Listen, Carly, you are great at this. You're smart, you could talk a client into buying a whorehouse if you wanted to, but…" (Hate that) "You're the most impatient person I have ever met. Sorry, but you're going to have to change."

We stared at each other.

"I have a present for you." I cooed.

She smiled. "You can't bribe me."

"Not a seminar! It's the holidays, Ellie, please? I'll change! New Years resolution. Very calm. Patient. Will not yell at customers. Promise." Ellie always was sending various agents to seminars. But no one on the planet that I had ever known was ordered to go to one called "*How to Make Simplicity and Patience the Cornerstones of Your Life*", on Friday three days before Christmas, causing me to nearly be hauled off the D.C. jail, and landing me in what I firmly believed was the worst traffic nightmare in U.S. history.

"I will get you back, Ellie. Just you wait," I sang loudly in the car, only I said 'wite' since I was mimicking Liza Doolittle in 'My Fair Lady', "'You'll be sorry but your tears will be too late. You be broke with all.." I stopped. This type of behavior was *not* following seminar rules.

Still stuck in the car, still in traffic, having progressed about an inch in the hour since the cop let me go; I found myself precariously creeping alongside the Potomac River, fantasizing that the monstrous four-wheeler with "Haz Mat" written on the side was going to veer left and shove me into the icy, black abyss where I would be trapped as the water crept up the sides of the windows and drowned me. I'd never see my children again. I'd miss all the Christmas parties we were invited to— not that my dreary husband, Paul, would be caught dead going to any of them because he became a hermit about a minute after I married him. Why did I marry him, I wondered. Oh that's right he looked great in ray bans.

But the situation regarding Paul had become alarming in the past months. My beloved nanny gave Paul a book on French impressionism for his birthday and the next day Paul announced he was taking a leave of absence from his job as a U.S. Air pilot in order to paint. He hadn't worked a day since. I'm not sure if it was the birthday or the book. No one else I knew had reacted so dramatically to turning thirty-nine.

Since then, Paul's crisp uniforms became a thing of the past. Instead he wandered around the house day after day in the same pair of blue jeans he had on the day I met him. They were a little faded. He wore button-down shirts, rumpled and un-tucked, with the sleeves rolled up. At dinner, he watched himself in the dining room mirror, practicing new dramatic gestures that, I assumed, he envisioned artists make. He caressed his hands as though they held some unbelievable creative power that might explode on canvas (if he had one) any minute.

I know *he* believed this new Paul was extremely sexy and deep. But when we kissed, which was more rare than birthdays, his stubble rubbed my cheeks like porcupine needles.

I made it across the bridge and into Georgetown. I thought I could practically jump out of the car, buy all the presents and hop back in at the rate the traffic was moving.

The traffic was loyal and stayed with me right on up to Massachusetts Avenue's intersection with Wisconsin Avenue next to the National Cathedral. This wasn't the most direct route to our house on the District side of Chevy Chase, but I tried to pass the cathedral whenever I was in the area. I stopped at the light, looked over, and gave it a salute. My brother, Timmy, and I used to salute each other all the time when we were kids. We had twenty different salutes—it was our own secret sign language. I can still remember them all. Eighteen years had passed since his memorial service was held in that cathedral, just three days after we'd scattered his ashes in East Hampton, Long Island, in the ocean by his favorite jetty—the second one of three on Georgica Beach. That's the way it should have been. After all, he died in it.

But I always gave a salute when I passed this sacred spot, this beautiful Cathedral, in case some of his spirit ended up there.

TWO

The kitchen was my favorite room in our house. I burned the last kitchen down with the toaster, so this one was only a year old. Two floor-to-ceiling windows overlooked the front yard. The floor and an island in the middle of the room were made of stained wood, and an antique rectangular table sat between the front windows. Bright pictures of animals, sailboats, and some things not quite recognizable painted by Kerry and Jamie filled the remaining walls. The best part was the fireplace with two small chairs and a tiny table. Kerry and Jamie sat there all the time, which I loved.

I studied the bright red and blue stars and stickers pasted on the two award charts that adorned our icebox. 'Aha!' I thought. 'Patrice's system of behavior modification was actually working; Jamie received a sticker for finding his library book. Maybe there was hope for him after all.' Kerry had ten stickers and Jamie had one. Kerry was meticulous. If I didn't remember screaming in agony giving birth to her, I'd swear she was adopted.

Kerry hated Christmas with a passion, which we all found unnerving. When she was five, during a Christmas party—*when we used to give parties*—a friend of Paul's, who hadn't left the keg's side all night for fear it might get up and walk away, dressed in a Santa outfit (a fake Santa, we keep reminding Kerry), entered her bedroom, thinking it was the bathroom. He had a beer in one hand, his beard was half off so that he could sip the beer, and as he walked in her room he took a pee all over her. Kerry woke up and saw this drunk and disorderly Santa lurking over her and she screamed and cried for hours. Even after she finally calmed down and we'd cleaned everything up, I sat there rocking her back and forth against her headboard; terrified she'd never be normal again, like a kid who witnessed a murder or something.

I poured a glass of wine and plopped down on a chair, putting off the family greetings for a moment. I could hear Jamie throwing a fit about having to take a shower and Patrice calming him down and cajoling him to wash his hair. I probably would have let him off the hook. But Patrice ran our house like Napoleon ran his troops, and Kerry and Jamie (and Paul and I) obeyed her. Everyone's room was neat. Every stitch of the children's clothing was labeled; they could go to camp in a flash and I wouldn't have to blink an eye.

Patrice. I lifted my glass and made a toast to her. "Thank you for giving me my life back. And don't you ever, ever leave! Hah!" I started to laugh, wondering how I had ever survived without her.

* * *

In the picture the Nanny agency sent me six months earlier, Patrice looked rather plain. That's exactly what I wanted—no one taller or prettier than me was living in *this* house. After fifteen years, marriage was hard enough. The references described Patrice (besides loving children, being cheerful, honest, etc.) as a "brilliant *organizer*." Aha! She sounded perfect. Patrice could find everything and put it someplace where it would be the next time we needed it.

I paid the agency, paid Patrice's ticket from Paris, and picked her up at Reagan National Airport all in the week in June that Paul was off on a five-day flying trip. Of course, I didn't dare ask Paul about a total stranger from another country coming to live with us because he would have given me the same answer he had since our honeymoon, NO. But, if I had a live-in nanny, Paul could no longer torture me with questions like, "why haven't you ironed my socks?" I thought this was something he secretly enjoyed. Power and control. Paul loved power and control and it was clear that in this marriage he had both.

So, I was a tiny bit worried about Paul's reaction to my drastic act of defiance as I hopped around restlessly like a cat on drugs at Reagan Airport in mid-June, all nervous and sweaty, swearing to myself I'd made the biggest mistake of my entire life and it would give ammunition for Paul to make the rest of my time on earth a living hell. "You did what?" he'd bellow.

"You couldn't manage keeping a house straight and being a good mother on your own? Carly, you stepped over the line, baby." He'd march into the study and slam the door, and I would live in terror until he'd act nice again.

Patrice was late. "I hate late people," I told some poor old lady standing next to me who'd been watching me with suspicion. I went into the restroom to throw water on my face because I was having an anxiety attack and then, remembering I might miss Patrice's arrival, darted out again and I saw her.

This nineteen-year-old, sultry, pouty, dark-haired French beauty swayed up the concourse at Reagan Airport, throwing her hair back every few steps in defiance of its rippling thickness and extraordinary length. Her four-inch, high-heeled black leather boots didn't even cause her to lose her stride, as I thought, certainly even at that age, I would have clumped a few steps and toppled over. Okay, she wasn't homely or short, but at least she wasn't blonde.

I tried to act normal as I greeted her, hoping she wouldn't notice the sweaty, trembling, red-faced wreck I was at the time. But Patrice seemed perfectly at ease from the minute she recognized me. She smiled broadly and waved, ran right at me to give me a hug and a kiss on both cheeks, dragged me to luggage, grabbed her things, and before I knew it, we were back at the house.

Five minutes later, Patrice was going through the whole place as if on inspection, taking everything out of drawers, closets, kitchen and bathroom cabinets, and desks. She demanded my attention and forced me to decide on the spot if something was to stay or be thrown out. I wanted to keep everything, so she gave up on me and did the whole thing herself. She did this for four days straight.

After that, I couldn't find anything, although everything was in perfect order.

There's something unsettling about having a French person around. It makes even fluent French speaking non-French people feel inferior; buying into America's conception that the French believe our country has no real culture. But Patrice was funny, lovable, and so energetic. Even the kids—Jamie, who was eleven, and Kerry, who was eight—adored Patrice from day one. Most likely, this was because they were fed on a consistent basis and could see the floors of their rooms.

Still, I became so anxious about Paul's arrival home that Patrice became my shrink a day after I met her. "You no let any man run your life. *He* has the easy life! You need to get strong, Mrs. Carly (I thought that was so cute), you need to show him that a woman has needs more important than his."

That's why French women were so colorful and happy. They went out to long lunches and drink fabulous wine while I had been stuck as a housewife for fifteen years.

"What is your husband's favorite thing to do when he arrives home from a trip?" Patrice asked.

"Drink dry martinis with four olives in his study and be left alone."

Patrice smiled.

When Paul arrived home, he walked in and out of the kitchen door, thinking he had gone to the wrong house. When he came back in, he was lead by Patrice (who introduced herself as "Patrice" and said nothing more) to his study where there was a Kettle One shaken-not-stirred "dirty martini" on a silver tray with ice in a silver bucket and the bottle of Kettle next to it. I think Paul had an orgasm when he walked in there. Wait until he sees the rest of the house, I thought. He'd really go over the edge.

And so just one week after her arrival, everyone in the house was in love with Patrice.

"DINNER!" Patrice's voice boomed through the house. No, it was booming in my ear, catapulting my brain back to the present. Actually, I'd heard it several times, but that may have been a dream. Reluctantly I opened an eye. Paul and Patrice were standing over me. I shut my eye.

"What shall we do?" Patrice asked.

* * *

"Oh, Lord, give the girl a bath or something. How the hell could she go to sleep in a dog bed?"

"It's immaculate," Patrice hissed at him. "I clean it every day."

"Oh, yes, so sorry." Paul was clueless. I was more awake.

"Do you suppose she's all right?" Patrice asked.

I opened my eyes. "I'm fine." I jumped up and flew past them to the bathroom, washed my hands, threw water and make-up on my face, brushed my hair, and hissed at the mirror, "You're a queen!" And then I started laughing at myself in the mirror, making all sorts of faces, so when I treaded softly into the dining room with shoulders back, Paul had filled my plate and was seated, waiting. He stood as I sat down—very gallant.

"Did you pass out?"

"I don't know."

"You went out drinking," Paul said accusingly.

"Give me a breathalyzer."

Silence. I looked at my plate of chicken, spinach, and a baked potato. The shadows of the candles looked scary against the wall. Paul's eyes were boring holes into me. I wanted to see my kids and snuggle with them in bed. The music playing throughout the house from Paul's ultra-sophisticated stereo system he'd given himself was creeping me out.

I took a bite of food and a sip of wine. Hmm. I felt a little better. "Do we really have to listen to a funeral march during dinner?"

SLAM went Paul's fork. He shot me a look and his eyes screamed, "How could you be so naïve? How could you not know that this is one of the best pieces of music ever created?" He slowly jabbed a grape and held it between his two front teeth, with his eyes narrowed, still staring into mine. I narrowed mine right back, mimicking him.

"I think it's time you learned to appreciate classical music, Carly. It's quite important," Paul informed me as if I was ten.

Merry fucking Christmas to you, too, asshole, I thought. But I smiled and chirped, "It's the holidays. I just thought we could listen to something a little more festive." I took another sip of wine and closed my eyes as if I were listening very carefully. "But, no, really, of course you are right, it's beautiful."

"Patrice studied music in Europe," Paul announced.

"She was born in Europe. It's a little different."

Clink, clink, clink. I sat there clinking my fork through the potatoes.

"I noticed you're ready for Christmas." Paul is on the attack now.

I responded brightly, "Voila. The tree!" We could see it in the living room all sparkly and gorgeous. I deserved major credit for this. I bought the thing, dragged it like a dead body into the living room, got it in that stupid plastic stand, and decorated it from head to foot.

"I think the key is to have presents underneath it. Jesus Christ, Carly."

"Wrong time of year to say that, don't you think?" I had to turn things around. No need for the evening to get nasty. I put down my fork dramatically, as if flustered and hurt. I sighed and stared at the floor.

There was a pause.

"Did you not see how exhausted I was, Paul? To fall asleep in a dog bed?" I let the shame sink in. "I was shopping for *you*, if you must know everything. Now it's practically ruined." At first I don't think Paul believed me, but I kept my pout. Then his lips widened into a grin and his eyes changed to playfulness.

"Give me a hint."

I shook my head firmly, playing our game. "Let's just say... have you been a good boy or bad?"

"Very bad." Paul raised and lowered his eyebrows.

I flipped my hair over half my face, licked my lips, and jiggled my boobs. "Be ready to prove it."

Paul laughed and in his Elvis voice went, "Oh *baby*, baby!" He sauntered over to me with his pelvis swinging. "Tell me about my present or I might have to tie you up."

I shook my head hard—the helpless heroine dying to get laid. "Never! No matter what you do to me!"

He took my wrists and put them behind my back. "Well, then, woman, I have no choice!"

The dining room doors flew open and the kids burst onto the scene almost as if Patrice had been eavesdropping on us to know the perfect moment.

Kerry was so clean her face shined. Her hair was still wet, making it look dark while allowing her eyes—sea green and almost exactly like Timmy's but rounder, slanting at the edges—to take center stage over blonde curls. Her walk, like the look in her eyes, was always a bit tentative, as if she thought she might step on a bomb.

"I hate showers. Why do I have to take them?" Jamie demanded, suddenly in my face. His brown, thick hair always stuck up straight at the crown, due to his cowlick, which was why he lived in baseball caps. It was wet, but the cowlick was growing with every second toward dryness. He kept fiddling with it, like it was an alien that lived on his head. He nearly climbed into my lap, but thought better of it. He was eleven and did not want to do anything babyish.

"Everyone takes showers, get over it," I told Jamie, a little harshly. "I'm just angry," I explained.

"Because you want to be good for Santa, That's why you take showers." Paul, standing awkwardly by the middle of the dining room table having almost gotten caught fooling around with his wife, of all people, announced to Jamie in a tone that echoed an insincere statesman.

'He's not six years old anymore.' I wanted to tell Paul.

Kerry looked at me with suspicion (at the mention of Santa), looping strands of her wet blonde hair around her ear—something she does when she's nervous. Paul read her and scooped her up. "Santa leaves the presents at Grandma's house, you silly goose," he told her, kissing her on the cheek. Kerry smiled, loving attention. "Although," he added, "Santa mentioned to me that he does have hurt feelings."

Kerry nodded absently, having heard that one before, and scrambled to get down. She came over and gave me a hug, pulling at Jamie's arm to go play, and he succumbed, rolling his eyes, because he was just too old for all this and too young to do anything else. And off they went.

"Have fun, love-birds," Jamie called back to us, and they both started snickering as they headed out the door. Paul and I just looked at each other.

Patrice floated down the stairs in a long black suede skirt that I could have sworn was mine, and she definitely smelled of my perfume. I didn't care. Besides, taking over all the chores and work I loathed with a passion, Patrice was the perfect buffer, and the jury was still out as to how the night would go.

"Patrice! Dinner was fantastic. We missed you," I told her.

Patrice leaned toward me and kissed each cheek. "Of course you did."

I laughed, loving her quickness.

"I was worried about you, Mrs. Carly, sleeping in Jackie's bed."

"Don't be ridiculous, Patrice," Paul told her, waving his hand like an artist would.

"Stop doing that!" I almost screamed. Instead we glared at him. Patrice folded her arms.

"You should go out and have fun tonight," Paul added, like he'd handed her a fifty.

"Oh fuck you, and apologize to your wife." Patrice waved her hand back at him. We all burst out laughing.

Paul looked at me, making his eyes droop. "I am so sorry, Mrs. Carly, I sounded quite harsh, and we are sooo worried about you." He burst into laughter, but Patrice and I just glared at him.

Paul's eyes told me "sorry" and he blew me a kiss. Then he came over and hugged me. "I love you, you know that," he whispered, and he kept holding me tight until the sting was gone. Things were either terrible or wonderful when we were around Patrice.

Patrice had slipped out of the room and returned with a bottle of wine from France; looking so triumphant you'd think she'd hunted the bottle down in battle. We cooed while she opened it.

Patrice made a face to Paul about the music and Frank Sinatra's Christmas carols blared over the stereo in about one second. Everything seemed suddenly gay and safe. Patrice's spirit knew how to glow on command and soon she and I started speaking French and dancing around, imploring Paul to join in, something he always refused to do; although, it was clear that he was enjoying himself. How could he not—with two flushed, flirtatious women teasing him so?

THREE

"Do NOT insult me with the pathetic excuse that you were drunk!" I was storming around the kitchen the next morning with the phone under my ear, listening to Paul explain that he drove Patrice "on a whim" to Georgetown and when he realized he couldn't drive home because of the strict drunk driving laws, he and Patrice had stayed at the Doubletree Inn.

"You went out to Georgetown with our nanny? And, spent the night with her?" Suddenly, this creepy feeling invaded my spine. "I mean, you got two rooms, right?"

"That would cost a fortune, Carly. Come on." He paused and laughed nervously. "Actually, you got off cheap. Patrice wanted to stay at the Ritz. She made a big scene about it."

Like I was the one who had lucked out here. I sighed. "Well, just come on home then." I could get past this. It wasn't a big issue, slightly strange, but no big deal. "We've got to get everything done for Christmas, Paul. You guys get back here. There's so much to do!"

There was a pause on the other line.

"I can't. You scare me when you're mad." Should I be mad? I thought I sounded desperate, not mad. Why weren't they on their way back? Paul didn't sound hurried in the least. That creepy feeling kept getting stronger—and then I knew.

There was a cloud of disbelief, like I was watching a movie in slow motion. Someone else was playing me, a wreck of a woman with a phone in one hand and a sponge in the other, cleaning bowls and throwing away miniature boxes of frosted cereal. One child was whining from upstairs that she couldn't find her blanket, the other was slinking out of the room after spilling a carton of orange juice all over the table, and her husband of fifteen years was in a hotel room with the only person she could really count on.

"You fucked her."

"Making passionate love is not fucking, Carly. And you know I don't like it when you use that word."

"That's great. Good fucking timing." It was all I could think of to say.

I dropped the phone and picked up my cup of coffee and smashed it on the floor. I left the broken pieces and got outside as fast as possible and ran around the back yard until I slowed to a march, before I started crying, kicking stones and pieces of dead wood as I paced around the yard the perimeter of our yard like a mental patient playing a prison guard. I had no idea what was happening. I couldn't comprehend it. It was too big to squeeze itself into my brain. It just could not be happening.

"It is not happening" I told myself, tromping through the uneven, un-cut, half frozen grass in a nightgown and drenched knee socks that, by the time I re-entered the kitchen to clean up the pieces of my favorite mug and try to decide how to calm myself down, were torn remnants of string.

I put the phone back on the hook and cleaned everything up before sitting on the floor rubbing my feet back to life, furious that Paul never mowed the lawn and the pile of wood was down to one piece and it was December. How would we have fires over the holidays? I wondered. How could all of us sit around the fireplace like a happy family when we had no fucking wood?

Maybe this affair had gone on right in front of me for months. Maybe Paul's whole leave of absence was to spend time with *her*. So, Patrice, Miss Angel-I-Love-You, was actually a seductive, calculating slut. It wasn't like she got raped. No police were knocking on the door. Oh, and she wanted to stay at the Ritz. "Patrice, you know how cheap Paul is, you stupid, lying bitch." I climbed up the stairs to Patrice's room to snoop around for clues but stopped stock still when I opened her closet.

It was like entering a wonderland. It was full of a multitude of colors and gauzy materials—flowing designer lingerie and silk robes, lacy bras, silk teddies, matching silk thongs with stockings and garter belts attached—all hung up meticulously with half of them still dangling price tags. As I inspected one three hundred dollar piece of material smaller than my thumb, I backed away. Paul? No! He was the cheapest man on the planet. But for great French sex? Who knows? How else could she possibly afford them? Paul was buying her these things. He had a trust fund. He could do things like this and I would never know.

I raced down to Paul's office, but all his credit card receipts and papers were locked in his little black safe. Of course.

I ran back up and threw all of Patrice's *old* things out the window and, feeling dissatisfied, smashed her alarm clock onto the driveway below.

The phone rang. I knew it would be Paul. Let it ring, I thought, let him be worried about me! He should be really worried. I thought. I had just decided to get his hunting gun out of the case and take it down to the Doubletree. Now, where did he put the key?

It rang and rang. The kids would pick it up eventually so I answered it.

"Things happen, Carly. Don't make it the end of the world. We'll be back later. I don't need a scene." And he hung up. I couldn't start screaming because of the kids. "Calm down. Calm down." I couldn't calm down

I locked the door to our bedroom and collapsed on the bed, punching the pillows and screaming into them as hard as I could.

Finally, I was exhausted, so I dragged my ugly, hung-over, bleary-eyed self downstairs to check on the kids—just as a car drove up. The feelings went from hope, anger, and confusion to the kind of hurt that almost kills you. Paul was crawling back to apologize, the horny shit. He'd be charming, contrite, bringing an early Christmas present, assuring me it meant nothing, that they had both drank too much and it was just an accident, and how he loved me and his family more than anything else in the world. Could we just forget it, honey? I heard him ask in my mind. Everything was ruined either way.

But it wasn't Paul in the car or Patrice. It was Alex. There was a stab of rage that it wasn't Paul, but Alex was almost better because he loved me no matter what. Dear, sweet Alex! Alex had been Timmy's best friend all of Timmy's short life, and then it was inevitable that he would become mine.

Alex had on his hospital greens, so he must have worked the night shift in the ER. The color complemented his Irish setter hair, fair and slightly freckled skin, and eyes so large and brown that I had secretly called him "Rhett" ever since I first met him when I was eight and he was eleven. However, his eyes had gradually deteriorated and he now wore glasses all the time and I couldn't read his thoughts like I used to. This can be a big disadvantage, not being able to see into someone's eyes.

"Hello, you gorgeous thing." Alex strode into my kitchen like a lion, like he could solve anything. He gave me a huge hug and swirled me around. Then he walked past me started calling out to the kids when I grabbed him.

"STOP!"

Alex turned around to face me but he wouldn't look at me. "Alex, I mean, you can't even talk to me?"

"Carly, we can later. I.. don't know what to say yet."

"Okay well.." The kids heard Alex and tumbled out from the living room where they'd been watching television to greet him. He announced, "I just came over because I was in the mood to cook pancakes and I thought, now who could I cook pancakes for?" They smiled. "Who loves pancakes? Mmm. Well, then it struck me. Kerry and Jamie Macalister, that's who!"

I folded my arms and gave him a look.

Kerry was clapping and hopping around like she'd never had a pancake in her life. "Can Alex make us pancakes? Can he? Can he, Mom?"

"Well..." I acted reluctant, playing along, even though I felt like screaming.

"Come on, Carly, I'm starving." Alex clutched his stomach dramatically and rolled his eyes, making his knees go weak as if he hadn't eaten in days. "Go on, out of my way, woman. Go take a bath or something."

Fine. I obeyed and climbed the stairs back to the refuge of my room; briefly noting that the mall expedition planned for later that day was looking precarious. 'It's not like I'm a child anymore, Alex. Things aren't so simple. You can't just make things better,' I thought. Hadn't Alex learned that when Timmy died? Paul screwing the nanny was nothing compared to that. Layering the pain with time, a husband, two children, healthy parents still alive and married to each other, and Alex always 'being there' did not take away from the fact that Timmy was dead. I had let nothing touch me since that happened. Nothing!

'And, what happens when you get married or move, Alex baby?' In fact, I was resentful that Alex was in my kitchen at all, thinking how long I had loved him and how, after all the dreams and longing, I still never knew what happened between us.

Hearing Alex's soothing voice in my kitchen brought me back to the first day I met him, playing neighborhood softball, when life was simple and the only thing I had to worry about was learning my multiplication tables that night. Alex's voice as he spoke with Kerry and Jamie sounded so much like it had that day, so long ago, when he was soothing *me*.

I'd had a serious crush on Alex since third grade when, on a spring afternoon, Timmy and I were playing softball and I noticed this new boy beside Timmy with flecked reddish hair and large brown eyes.

"Slugger, you're up!" Timmy called to me. He'd endured after hours of practice with me so I could play. I stood up with Timmy's favorite bat, thought about the adorable red-haired boy watching, let the first pitch go like I'd been taught to, and then walloped the next one into a homerun.

As I ran the bases, Timmy was screaming and hollering, "That's the way to go! Yes! Go, Carly Russell, go!" Timmy was ecstatic, since he had taught me exactly how to play. (He had no choice because I followed him everywhere—like Piglet followed Pooh.)

We won the game. I was kind of a hero. Timmy asked Alex over. I tried to settle down at the kitchen table to learn my multiplication when Alex sat down to help me. I liked his red bangs stuck to his damp forehead.

Timmy scrounged around the cabinets for some cookies or chips to sneak before dinner and hopped around making fake soccer goals while Alex helped me with multiplication and long division. Both of them were wearing blue and white shorts, long green socks, soccer shoes and blue shirts with numbers on the back from playing real soccer before our pick-up softball game. Their faces were red and moist from both; the backs of their shirts were damp, and their legs had streaks of dirt caked on their knees and socks.

"Mrs. Silverspoon always tests on nine times nine," Alex informed me.

"I actually know them. I'm smart," I blurted out before realizing how stupid that sounded.

"That's good. Oh…" He put out his hand. "My name is Alex."

Was he laughing at me? I couldn't look at him to see. I started scribbling on a piece of paper again. He stayed for dinner.

And after that day, Alex came over nearly every afternoon. Alex secretly used his friendship with Timmy as an excuse to see me. He never said that, but I was sure of it. By the time I was ten, my very best friend Tina and I planned our double wedding: she would marry Timmy and I would marry Alex. The boys didn't seem committed to the plan, but Tina and I figured we had plenty of time to work on them.

Tina and I attended the National Cathedral School, which was the sister school of St. Albans and located on the same campus, right where Wisconsin Avenue and Massachusetts Avenue intersected, on a slight hill high enough to see the whole city. In the middle of both campuses was the National Cathedral, which was so awesome that, when I was a little girl, it gave me total faith that God was watching over me. I'd sneak in there all the time and talk directly to Jesus. We had a special friendship. Or at least I thought so until he took away my brother and it took me ten years to even speak to him again. He was the one who screwed up the friendship, I thought. But as I grew older he kind of slipped back into my life.

From the day I met Alex, my life became more of a fantasyland than before, which, though unreal, had both wonderful and frightening parts. From as far back as I remember (around three years old) my memories contained excitement and fear. Mom floating out in evening dresses, Dad backing some brand new shiny Cadillac—or whatever the latest brand of car had come on the market (he loved cars and planes)—so carefully out of the garage that Mother had already lost her temper with impatience by the time he had pulled up to the front door.

'They're leaving again. Please take me with you! You expect Timmy to tuck me into bed again?' I pleaded to them with my eyes. I loved Timmy, but his methods of caring for me were a little careless. The careless ones were my parents for leaving us so young. Off they'd go to the White House, the embassies, a dinner dance, or a speech Dad was giving with a reception following at the Metropolitan Club. But when Mom gave parties, life was at its best – Timmy and I in our pajamas watching between the staircase posts as Secret Servicemen would "precheck the home" to the point where they'd even taste Mom's dinner. 'The President was coming! The President was coming!' It always gave you a funny feeling in your stomach from excitement and wonder. But the best part was that I knew my parents weren't going out that night. They were having the party so they weren't going anywhere. And I could see them all glamorous and happy and gay. Looking back I realized they really didn't go out often at all – maybe once a week. But for some reason, it made the house feel so strange and big that even with Timmy there, it felt unsafe to me.

Sometimes Dad would be on television or in the paper and was referred to as a man with "integrity and diplomacy." Mom was always in the society section, a glamour girl former model who'd a fascination of Washington's society. I hated that. I wanted her to pay attention to **me**.

By Middle School I didn't really care, because Timmy and Alex still went to school on the same campus as mine. It made every day exciting. I'd run into them in the hallway, in the lunch line, at all of their sports games, and they actually came to all of mine, which was the main reason I made four varsities in tenth grade. And Alex spent nearly every minute at our house. Who needed parents around when you were in love?

But after Timmy died, everything went south. Everything.

"Fuck them both," I said to Jackie the Jack Russell puppy, who lay asleep beside me on my bed as I was jarred back to the present with the sound of Kerry's laugh, not exactly sure who I was talking about.

FOUR

I took a shower and went down to the kitchen. The kids were gone—back to their games. I wanted a game to put me in another world, I thought.

Another car roared up the driveway. My sixty-nine-year-old mother leaped out of her Thunderbird convertible (she had the top down and it was thirty-three degrees outside), raising her hand in apology. Mom knew never to come over without calling, because I'd told her not to. My parents lived five minutes away. Sometimes it felt too close, sometimes too far.

"I cannot believe this," I panicked, clutching Alex. "Tell her anything. Tell her I'm throwing up and she has to leave!"

"She won't fall for that."

I had to agree, so we went outside to greet her. Mom had a way of springing when she walked, as if with the next step she'd fly off into the air. She used to leap out of her sports car without opening the door, but Dad and I held an intervention so she gave that up.

"My dear girl. I called you five times with no answer. I thought you were either dead or lost." She looked me up and down. "Carly Macalister, you look like you just crawled out of a grave." She cupped my cheeks. "Are you okay?"

Alex swooped into her radar. "Carly's fine. She looks awful, but…"

I swung around. "Fuck you."

"Alex! Merry Christmas!" Mom's entire being lifted. "Just the man I wanted to find. You're coming to Christmas dinner, of course, right?"

"I'd be honored."

"Were you two kissing?" Mom beamed at us, loving a conspiracy. "I mean, God, you look gorgeous together. I always thought it should be the two of you who got married instead of you, Carly, marrying that ass-ho.."

"No, Mom. Alex just cooked breakfast." I told her in my 'shut up' tone. It was not the occasion to hear this little lecture.

Mom glared at me. "Well," she huffed. "One can only dream." If she hadn't been saying the same thing to us ever since I married Paul and Alex returned from the west coast, Alex and I would have been embarrassed. She was smart, though, because, since I was married, it was all kind of a joke, the kind that hold the truth underneath, as jokes tend to do.

Mom spotted some of Patrice's clothes that had missed the lawn and lay in the driveway. "Did Patrice fall out of the window?" she asked.

"It is so sweet of you to come by!" I announced in a high, false voice, attempting to lead her back to her car. Mom was waving her hand to resist.

"Kerry just called. She wants new tennis shoes for Christmas."

"Hers are fine. They're just a little worn. She's a perfectionist."

Mom turned and looked me up and down. "Aren't genes fascinating?" Then she tried to get past me, peering over my shoulder at the kitchen door. "Can't I go inside? I promise I won't look at a thing. I just need six wine glasses and I'm out of your hair. Plus I'm your mother and I think you're hiding something from me."

"Mom," I tried to steer her back to the car, "the last time you were here at Christmas you broke your leg. And we haven't fixed the steps yet. Go home and I'll bring the glasses later."

At least three times around Christmas, Mom had ended up in the hospital: twice for anxiety and once when she broke her leg on the steps of my house hurrying us all to church. Dad and I took her to the emergency room and the doctor believed she had fallen as a result of "extreme exhaustion and nerves." He had glared at all of us when he said this.

"Well," she sounded hurt, "when Kerry called, I asked the kids over for the night. I told them they could open one present each. I thought you could use the time to wrap."

"Oh, I'm all done."

Everyone laughed.

I studied her for a few moments, watching her speak with Alex in a vain attempt to avoid being sent home to "the most boring man that ever drew breath" (my father), her arms flying off in different as she spoke, a body always animated, never listless, matched with a spirit that just can bowl a person over with its sheer force. Her black, thick hair was tied back with a black velvet ribbon. She was wearing huge sunglasses, like a movie star determined to protect her privacy. Despite a drastic series of knee injuries resulting from skiing out of control over cliffs, trees, other unfortunate people (even the skiers in line who watched in terror as she careened closer and closer, scrambling to get out of Mom's way as she plowed into a few of them and practically decapitated herself from the rope line), she still hopped around all over the place – stores, parties, friend's houses, the kids' school, I mean I have never known a human with more energy. Ever since she was forced to stop skiing, (a fact she still refuses to entirely accept which is why we all play the twisted game of denying it) her only interest is in one person: me.

At that moment, I realized my only goal in life was to get rid of my mother, and if it meant loaning out the kids, then fine. I asked Alex to get the glasses and then dragged Kerry upstairs to pack a quick bag, peeled Jamie from Nintendo so he could do the same, ordered them into Mom's car, and kissed them goodbye.

Alex followed me back inside after I waved them off.

"I don't have any presents. I'm going to have to go to the fucking mall," I said. I was balancing myself on Kerry's stool, attempting to feel around the top of the hall closet for wrapping paper. "Damn. I was sure I put it there. And I can't go look in the attic. It has rats. Or bats. They clunk around right above my bed, as if any minute they'll break through the ceiling and eat me alive. Paul promised he'd do something about them, but..."

Alex was watching me the way you might watch someone who's just been in a really bad car accident and doesn't know it yet, but her neck is broken. It was a look of pity, a look that swept across his face and was gone, but I caught it and found it revolting. Lust would be good. Not pity. Oh well, what did I expect? I just got cheated on by my husband with my nanny. I'd pity me too.

"And what in the world am I going to get my mother?" I hopped off the stool, my back toward him so face to face would not be happening at that raw moment – the pinnacle of humiliation. I scrambled through the kitchen drawers looking for tape I had used to put up the kids' drawings. Paul and I had finished lists of what we were going to get each child. Order.

Paul loved order. Not that one thing had actually been bought yet, but it was a start. "You know I have to get something great for Mom."

There was silence. Silence at a time like this needed to be filled.

"I got your parents a trip to Paris," Alex blurted out.

"WHAT??" I turned around, furious. Alex was all flushed and he backed away a step. "How dare you? I can never beat that! Plus Dad will never go. He might go, I guess, but I mean—" Then I had the perfect solution. "Will you share the present with me? We'll give it to them together. It will be great!" I smiled and lunged forward to hug him. He looked terrified, which I thought was a bit over the top.

"No! I can't do that, Carly. Your parents have taken care of me my entire life and I can finally afford to give them something really fantastic." He paused. "You understand that, right?"

I turned back to the drawer. "Give it to them in private, then. You don't need to upstage everyone at Christmas." I was cool. Hurt and cool. "It would be the ideal Paul-revenge, but if you want to be selfish…"

Dad should be buying her the trip to Europe. Nothing was making any sense.

I couldn't find any tape, but I did come across a pair of children's scissors. "Aha!" I came into the living room. "I'm making progress."

"Carly, I'll get the tape, wrapping paper, and some decent scissors. Just come in the living room and stop moving for a moment."

So I did. He was standing there, unsure of what he could say or do to make it easier. Mr. Fix-it. I thought about everything he'd already done—making the kids happy with pancakes, taking on my mother, helping me with Christmas, being there for me when he had no sleep after a long night in the ER—and I thought about how I'd adored him since I was eight years old because he always protected me, even from my family, from Timmy when he got manic and from my parents when they were too self-absorbed in Washington society and its seduction to really watch out for a little girl.

"Will you spend the next year or so here, until I adjust?" I asked.

Alex smiled his ironic way and gave me a hug. It felt so good that I thought this might be a really good time to finally have sex with him, but I knew his face would turn into a tomato and he'd actually catapult himself from my embrace, and I'd had enough rejection for one day. You just couldn't act suddenly outside the box with Alex. I did all the time, but that was different because we were *friends*. But Alex was weird when it came to girlfriends. His last girlfriend did something complicated and scary, like borrow his blow dryer, which entailed opening up one of his cabinets, and she was history.

"Now, you haven't wrapped a thing, right?" Alex asked, letting me go.

"Nope. Haven't bought a thing, either." I looked around. "I know, let's have champagne!" Escape from reality had always held a special appeal to me.

"Carly, I don't think..."

The phone rang. I pounced on it. "Yes?"

"Can we just forget this? I do love you, Carly. It's just I don't think I love you *enough.*"

Okay, Paul, you're off the hook. I pointed to the kitchen and whispered to Alex, "The champagne. It's urgent."

"So you go fuck my nanny? That's a *hateful* thing to do and you are a huge fucking fucked up asshole to have done it." I wanted to *kill him*.

Alex walked in with one glass of champagne. "Carly, are you sure you want to drink this? It could make you feel worse," he whispered.

"Fuck you, too" I told Alex, grabbing the glass, despising his patronizing attitude that bordered on superiority.

"Good. I hear Alex." Paul was feeling proud. He'd taken care of the situation by calling Alex.

"Yes, and we're in bed fucking, so if you could get to the point…"

"Carly!" Alex was mortified.

"I don't think it is wise for me to see you right now," Paul's stern voice echoed over the phone. "I just wanted to let you know that Patrice and I are going to go buy all the children's presents, since we know you are incapable of accomplishing this."

I covered the phone. "Alex, I was kidding," I mouthed. "Sorry."

Alex glared at me.

"Of course," I told Paul.

"I told you never put me in the middle," Alex hissed.

"You can manage to get presents for your own family, I assume?" asked Paul.

"Of course." Then to Alex, "Christ, Alex, everyone knows you're too scared to get near me."

"We'll follow Kerry and Jamie's lists. I think they'll be pleased." Paul sure seemed pleased.

"Of course. I'm sure they will." To Alex (all in whispers), "You just love the fucking game."

"You're married, remember?" Alex's face was all flushed. "That was your choice, not mine."

"Would you stop saying that?" asked the phone.

"Saying what?" I was confused.

"'Of course.' Stop saying that."

"Of course I will," I assured Paul. Then to Alex, "My choice? Right. You ran away, remember?"

"You could at least thank us for doing your job for you," Paul lectured. Alex turned to leave, so I threw the phone on the couch and followed him while the phone kept on lecturing. "Patrice understands what I'm talking about," I heard it say, thinking, "Patrice understands that seducing and eventually marrying what she perceives as a rich American with a house in Chevy Chase is the way to go. Then she could hire her *own* nanny."

Alex and I faced each other in the kitchen, emotions on the rim.

"I go to Stanford Med and you run off and get married like a childish brat."

I took a breath. "I waited for you all my life!" I shouted.

"Right. From third grade to twelfth."

"So you *did* think of me as a child the night Timmy died. Timmy was right all along." I crossed my arms.

"No," Alex replied slowly, "I think you're acting like one now." He turned and calmly walked out the kitchen door.

If Timmy were still alive, we'd be doing a snow dance outside, or having an outdoor barbecue in thirty- degree weather, or dancing in Georgetown to a live band, or out on a boat in the middle of the Potomac, two nights before Christmas, running Christmas lights up her mast and sailing her up the river.

FIVE

Jackie, my Jack Russell, and I spent the next few hours having quality time. I was hugging her and sobbing and she lay patiently in my arms, sleeping while I told her everything. The afternoon wore itself into darkness, as it has a habit of doing in December. "I hate it when it isn't daylight savings time," I told Jackie.

It started to rain, only harder. The weather reports had predicted either rain or snow. Finally I crept down into the basement to get out Jamie and Kerry's sleds, just in case the rain might turn to snow during the night and we could wake up to a white Christmas Eve. That would cheer anyone up.

I found Jamie's gloves. Kerry wouldn't wear gloves because she thought her fingers might get lonely, and I never wanted any part of Kerry to be lonely. I couldn't find her mittens. I would have to make a list so I could ask Patrice where everything was. That should be fun. I'd be kind of like the ousted first ladies who, after a two-year (why were they so long, those campaigns? It's ridiculous, I thought, as my mind wandered everywhere to avoid thinking about one particularly glaring problem) vicious campaign, were forced to smile and give the incoming wife a tour of the White House.

I was still in the basement fooling around when the door-bell rang, which made me shriek involuntarily and jerk straight upright, knocking my head on a pipe. It could be anyone. It could be Paul. What would I say? I couldn't let him see me—I looked like an unraveled ball of thread. I had forgotten to blow-dry or even comb my hair, the mascara had dripped down my cheeks from crying, I was in the process of putting on one of Patrice's red lace super-sexy teddies (that reached the middle of my thigh because Patrice was so tall) with matching old-fash-ioned stockings I had grabbed off the line of rope where she had laid them to dry. Paul had been supporting her like a hooker, I was sure, spending the money supposedly saved for his family. I almost tore the thing in shreds, but I put the whole get-up on instead—struggling with the stockings in the half-black base-ment, swearing, hopping around on one leg and then the other, bent over so I wouldn't hit the pipes—when I had the insane compulsion to put on one of my ski boots lying in a pile, in order to remember that I was very good at something and no one could take that away from me. Then the doorbell rang, but I couldn't get the boot off that quickly.

No, Paul definitely couldn't see me like this.

It rang again. Jackie the Jack Russell was barking like a German shepherd, which was comforting. If it was a robber, let's say, or an ax murderer, he'd turn around and run. I'm pretty sure everyone is scared of German shepherds.

"Carly? Open the damn door!" Tina, my best friend in the entire world, screamed from outside.

I climbed the stairs slowly and hunched over, clomping up with my ski boot, watching my shadow reflected on the wall like something out of an Alfred Hitchcock movie. Alfred Hitchcock himself. Slump, slump, slump. Or, I could have been in the basement for days, making evil potions. Slump, slump. "Come in, come in," I called out in an evil-sounding voice, pretending I was a witch.

Tina got tired of waiting and burst through the door. She looked almost exactly the same as she did fifteen years ago, when she was maid of honor at my wedding. Her hair was still dyed red, although she'd cut it into short spikes and some of them were purple. She had on a suede mini-skirt with a black tank top underneath a black leather jacket. She also had on her typical black fishnet stockings and black leather boots that came up to her calf. Tina always wore three-inch high heels even in August, except when she was wearing her bikini. The boots put her at five feet three inches. She was carrying a huge duffel bag.

"Bearing gifts for the divorcee?"

"No, you moron, they're presents for your family." Tina looked me up and down. "Nice outfit. Do you know how hard it is to shop for your mother? I finally ended up getting her a tiara. Isn't that perfect? I'd show you, but it's wrapped." Alex had obviously passed the buck and called her. I had been planning to call her, I just didn't know how.

She planted the bag down, which took over the entire kitchen table. I sat down on the floor and struggled with my ski boot.

"I'm spending the night," she announced.

"It looks like you're staying for a month." That sounded mean. "Which I would love," I added.

"I told you, they're *presents*. You can pay me back next year. I brought Chinese too." Tina had the wine glasses out and was pouring wine. Oh well, why not? "I also got your mother a make-up kit. And black leather driving gloves too. Isn't that perfect?" Tina and Mom were both very dramatic and, in this way, they understood each other.

"It's perfect," I said. "Help me get this thing off." I was on the floor, wrestling with the boot. "I can't take off this fucking outfit until I get the fucking boot off."

Tina started pulling as hard as she could, rocking the ski boot back and forth, when she suddenly lurched forward and hugged me. I stiffened a little, surprised.

"Paul's a shit. He always has been. And Patrice can't hold a candle to you, Carly." Then she studied me. "You look great as a hooker. Promise!" Tina had apparently given up on the boot and was up again, unloading Chinese take-out, wrapped presents, CDs, cigarettes, and videos. "You just got married too young. How could you know?" was her take on it.

Tina always wanted to be a psychologist. She ended up at a public relations firm for musicians and artists. She says it's almost the same thing. "Twenty-one years old! Carly, you were just a baby when you married that jerk." My face was sweaty from overexertion.

"I got Jamie hockey skates," she continued. "Perfect, right? Stop fiddling with that boot. Your foot will swell and you'll never get it off." She handed me a glass of white wine and sat next to me on the floor, in her shrink mode. "Truly, honey, you look a little strange. Are you okay?"

I wanted to claw the boot off and tear Patrice's underwear off as well. "I was just trying to cheer up," I explained.

Tina had gotten the fireplace poker and was trying to pry my foot free when Paul and Patrice walked in. Patrice was sheet white and looked quite regal in my skirt and her twelve-inch-tall suede boots, towering over me as I cowered on the floor. She started screaming at me in French. One hand clutched her wet clothes, which she then threw all over the floor, and in her other hand were pieces of her smashed clock, which she smashed down on the floor in a fury as well. This was very French: they were constantly using their hands for emphasis.

I thought she was going to lunge on top of me when she noticed that I was wearing her clothes and started screaming in French much faster and louder. I covered my head for protection as she towered over me. Even Tina looked nervous and got out of her way. Fair weather friend.

"What the hell is she saying?" Paul wanted to know.

"She's *your* goddamn girlfriend, you tell me!" I screamed at him.

Tina started translating like a reporter, "Patrice says, 'How could you? You are a terrible bitch. These are my things you ruined. I am distraught. This is terrible…my beautiful things…this is despicable. And you are wearing my beautiful new clothes. But I would forgive you if you hadn't destroyed my beautiful clock. You will go straight to hell.'"

The confusion felt refreshing. I didn't feel empty anymore.

"Hey, let's get the kids over. We could have a party!" I shouted over Patrice to Paul. He briefly smiled, his expression mixed with regret, pity, love, sadness. We held each other's eyes.

Of course there were slices of heaven with us in the little things—Sundays by the Potomac with the kids on bikes, when Jamie darted straight into the Potomac River and I raced in to retrieve him; picnics next to the landing strip where I'd meet Paul after one of his flying trips and we'd lie flat, watching the planes practically touch us as they landed; our favorite restaurants downtown, bopping around to different nightclubs before Jamie and Kerry were born; the way he looked in his uniform kissing me goodbye; wrapping up in sleeping bags and making kinky, fun love by the fire after we'd gotten through Jamie's scare with low blood platelets which could have led to tons of horrible things; the roses he brought me every year on the anniversary of Timmy's death; Paul playing airplane with the kids and flying them around on his shoulders right before they went to bed; the parties we gave when I cooked Italian food; setting Tina up for about fifty disastrous dates and watching in wonder at her outrageous antics; the night we got robbed and I chased the burglar away and he tackled me on our bedroom rug and we made love until morning; the few times we talked until dawn…

But it was like trying to hold back a tidal wave. It was coming, there was nothing you could do, but delaying made it easier to take, might even diminish it to just a really large wave with not a great deal of power, one you could actually dive through and swim safely out the other side.

Then it all hit me. "Fuck both of you. You lying, conniving, horrible people whom I trusted and loved more than anyone and you go do this to me? You go and leave me right before Christmas, right when we're all supposed to love each other, and Paul, you take away my whole life and all the love we had in this family for some fucking conniving French whore? You're going to ruin everything for her? Fuck you! I hate you! You and that thumb of a dick destroyed your children, our whole lives, for a fuck? You asshole! And you…" My eyes were narrowed, my temper was out of control, and now Patrice was cowering. I approached her, knowing in some part of my mind that she couldn't understand all the words, but then again the lying bitch probably could, "You are the slimiest of all! Pretending you are my friend, taking perfect care of MY CHILDREN who I trusted you with, and thinking this will be your life? Well, let me tell you, you little French clueless slut, after it is all over and you think you've gotten him, you'll realize he is cheap. Do you hear me??"

I was screeching in her ear and she was cornered now from backing away and kind of slinking lower and lower, and I couldn't stop, "you will be a miserable, lonely, broke, hated bitch! No one in this city will be your friend! My mother will make sure of it! You. You lying, fucking…" I couldn't go on. I just couldn't. It was all too sad, too horrible, too real, too much. I turned and ran upstairs and locked the door, flinging myself once again on my bed, screaming into those pillows until I couldn't cry or scream anymore.

Of course, the safest thing would be to stay on the beach, stay in the marriage, and make it all work, stay still, and stay flat. It was up to Paul, and I realized suddenly that I hadn't had a voice in the marriage from the beginning. And, by choosing Patrice, he had all his power back, and then a tiny voice in the back of my head reminded me that I did have a fighter instinct, and that even though Paul was winning the battle, it could be a long war.

When I came downstairs they were gone. Tina and I went into the living room. "I got your father golf balls. You do that every year, right?" she tried to chirp cheerfully. "Three hours and I got everything. I deserve a kiss."

I gave her a kiss. We picked up our glasses and cheered silently, because we didn't know what to toast.

Paul arrived the next morning in freshly ironed clothes I'd never seen before. I wondered if he had bought *her* a new outfit too. He didn't call first. He just arrived. It was Christmas Eve.

When I was planning Paul's funeral last night, I envisioned the entire occasion. I'd be dressed in a brand new black dress. I'd look like Kate Moss. A tragic waif. The bereaved widow. But Paul didn't look like he was going to die any time soon. And I knew I didn't have the nerve to shoot him. But it had passed the night.

Paul finally rang the doorbell. I waited a moment. He rang it again. I stood on the other side.

"Who is it?" I asked.

"It's Paul, Carly," he answered gravely.

"Paul who?" I asked.

"Jesus, will you open the door, please?"

"What's the password?"

I could hear him whisper something like, "shit." I opened the door.

He walked past me without a word and headed upstairs; presumably to retrieve anything he had left. *Hey, your whole life is here, remember?* A minute later he came back down with his electric toothbrush. Then he went into his study and lugged his black metal file cabinet out to his car so I couldn't break it open and find out how much money he'd spent on other women. I wondered how many other women. He wasn't acting like this was the first time.

I was scribbling on a piece of paper, trying to make a "To Do" list, when he came back into the kitchen.

"I'll meet you at your parent's tomorrow morning. I'll go early and unload the presents for the kids."

"Cool," I said. I kept scribbling. I was making smiley faces. Patrice had always gone to her cousin's for Christmas, so her plans wouldn't be affected in the least, I thought bitterly. I was surprised Paul didn't insist on going with her.

"Carly, can you put that down? You know how I hate that. You're always scribbling."

I put the pen down.

"I'll come to your parents' for Christmas breakfast, but I can't go for dinner. It would be too much."

"You've never come to the dinner part."

He sighed. "That's true. You always said you understood."

"I do. It's fine," I said, thinking it was a ridiculous subject to dwell on. Everything was different now. He even looked different. I noticed his hair was shot through with gray. Had it been before? I couldn't remember. He didn't move from the door, as if he wanted to say something else. I waited.

"I want to take the kids to Disney World after Christmas. I still have four U.S. Air passes, so they can go free. My entire family is going. You can't say no."

"Why didn't you mention this before?"

"Because I didn't want to go with *you*," he explained.

I had been trying to get him to take us all to Disney World for three years. My face felt cold. I tried to remember that seminar. *Count to three, take deep breaths, don't yell, and don't lose control.* But all I felt like was a child whose parents left for an outing and came back three hours late, but it seemed like three years.

"What a divine idea."

"Patrice thought it would be an ideal solution. The kids always wanted to go and…"

"Do you guys use sign language to communicate?"

"You said you'd act like an adult!" His voice was rising.

"I never said any such thing!"

Suddenly we were both quiet, because this wasn't how either one of us wanted it to go. Then, very slowly, as if he'd memorized the words, he said, "I have tickets for the twenty-sixth. I thought of this last night. I didn't get any sleep. I just thought it would be best for the kids to have a great vacation before…before we make any decisions. Any major ones."

I picked up the pen and started scribbling again. I never could listen unless I was doing something else. He ignored it. "They love their cousins. And it'll give us some time."

I stood up and walked past him out the kitchen door. I needed space, and fresh air.

"You can say you have to work," he called after me. He had it all figured out. "It'll give you a chance to, you know, adjust. Come on, Carly; tell me you haven't been miserable too. I made a bad mistake, but you know what? I can't stand the way things are with us. You know?" He was behind me, so I kept walking out to the back yard. I wanted him to go away.

"We have two kids! We have to try," I shouted, still walking.

"Everything I loved about you drives me crazy now," he explained. I turned around. At least he was being honest. But I felt suddenly sickish, like when you drink a beer really fast and you can feel it all the way to your toes. "Come on, Carly, Patrice was a blip on the radar screen. You know I've been having affairs for years. You're not a child. What do you think pilots do?"

I bent over. No, I had not known. I must have been the dumbest human being in the entire world. "Jesus, Carly, you have to admit, our sex life is a *joke*. How can I be attracted to someone who can't do a damn thing right? Your whole life was a disaster until Patrice.

"I did everything! I stayed home and did everything while you were off fucking stewardesses!"

"Flight attendants," he corrected me. "Actually, I like hookers. I'm a sex addict. Not that you'd ever notice. You're about as adventurous as a—"

That's when I turned around and slugged him. I didn't mean to. He actually reeled and almost fell down. I thought I had broken my hand. We both just stood there, shocked. He steadied himself on our new white picket fence. It had been my dream to have one and now it was holding up my husband, who I had just socked.

"I think you need some professional help," he finally said and turned to walk to his car. He got in and started it. He got back out again as I was walking toward the house.

"Most men are just like me, Carly, they just don't admit it. You're living in another goddamn century!"

"I'm fucking gorgeous!"

"You haven't turned me on since Jamie was born. Sorry, honey." He was enjoying this. "I want to take the children to Disney World. I have two rooms. Patrice is coming as a nanny. She's just coming to help me."

"I could have helped you," I shouted at him. "I know the kids pretty well, remember? Let's see, what are their names again?"

He was maddeningly calm. "I need to know in the next few hours, Carly. I got the last four seats. They're reserved until midnight."

I turned and kept walking.

"Think of the kids," he called out. I was at the door. Then I heard him say, "Christ, I think you broke my nose. Jesus." He started the car and pulled down the driveway, never looking back.

I escaped to the bathroom and started running the tub to drown out the world. I'd never hit anyone before. Ever. I had never hit the kids. My boss was concerned about my temper because I got impatient with buyers when they made stupid decisions. But they always thanked me afterwards. They appreciated it, and that's why I did well.

I'm smart. People like me. I'm successful. I'm lovable. I kept telling this to the mirror, as it got steamier. Finally I could barely see myself. My hand ached. It was all red. I was shaking. I wanted to break the glass on the steamy mirror. I wanted to shatter everything. I wanted to shatter his smugness. I wanted to shatter his coldness, his disdain, his condescending voice, his flirtations with waitresses, his way of always looking at himself when we passed a store window, his moodiness, his inability to reach for me, his withdrawal, the fact that he hated it when he couldn't find matching socks, that he closed his study door for hours just because I'd lost something. It could be a pen. It could be an earring. It didn't matter. I had lost it.

It occurred to me: What if he wanted to take the kids forever? A week could turn into longer. They could love their new candy daddy. They could think it would be safer with him. He could plant that thought in their heads. He and Patrice could do it so easily. The kids might think I couldn't handle it. They could choose to live with him. He had money that would always be there. I'd have to work and be there when I could.

The bath was too hot to get into. I had no one to call. I wasn't ready to face anyone, even Tina; even she wouldn't understand. But she was up, and I could hear her in the kitchen, rummaging around, trying to find something. I took my bath, dressed, and went down to see her.

Tina thought I should let them go. The kids would have a fantastic time. Did I want to deprive them of the trip of their dreams? Think of them. Blah, Blah, Blah.

"Life is uncertain. Eat dessert first," I told her. Let them go, I decided. They might not get another chance.

SIX

Tina and I left to finally go buy presents, just a tiny bit "last minute." I drove down to the quaint small shops in Georgetown and bought the kids a few things Patrice and Paul wouldn't know they wanted just to exert a little control, just to be part of the process. While Tina was in Clyde's (our favorite pub) devouring a burger and flirting, I strode down a few streets to the store where she'd fallen in love with a purple mini-skirt I wouldn't be caught dead in. Tina was a size one. The sales lady looked at me doubtfully until I asked for it to be gift-wrapped. At least I didn't have to worry about buying anything for Paul and Patrice, which was a huge relief. There's a bright side to everything.

Tina and I met up again and I took side roads out of Georgetown, rattling down cobblestone streets, passing antique churches and tiny town homes just beginning to glisten with Christmas lights as dusk approached. Thank God Tina was with me. I needed some of her spunk to rub off on me. Tina had been rebellious since the moment I met her at age six, when she stole one of her dad's cigarettes and came over to my house to see if I wanted to try it. Her crush on Timmy began that very day. Some people just start thinking about the opposite sex earlier than others, and Tina was definitely one of those. I know, at least in the beginning, she came over all the time because of him.

When we got to be teenagers, Tina went completely wild. At seventeen she married a drummer in a local band (she was the singer for a while. She was actually quite good.) She wore outrageous costumes and loved to be the center of attention. But the marriage only lasted six weeks. Afterwards, she arrived back home broke and with a severe cough and fever. She looked like a person could blow her over with one breath and she'd be dead.

Tina had her wacky over-the-edge side, but she was always there for me. When her parents moved to California she stayed here, at least in part because she knew the reason they had moved in the first place was to get away from her. I think they finally just didn't know what to do with her. I'd just had Jamie and she was the godmother. She stayed with us for a few months before she got the apartment she still lives in, a huge loft on the seventh floor with a view of the cathedral and a lovely doorman. Sometimes I wished I could have just lived with her. Paul couldn't stand it when Tina lived with us. Maybe he felt left out. He's never had a friendship like that.

I was almost lulled into the Christmas spirit with Tina singing Christmas carols at the top of her lungs, and since she had been in a band and I had no radio, they sounded good to me.

Then we hit Rockville Pike, a monotonous world jammed with cars, faceless superstores, and chronic red lights. Anywhere, Suburbia. Tina thought it was time to go back to the house and take a nap. Easy for her to say, she had no family and I still had my mother to worry about. This thought made me extremely sad and I started crying uncontrollably. Here Tina was, being my very best friend, and she had no one to buy presents for because she had no family? Tina couldn't get me to stop crying.

"You need food," she told me firmly, patting my back like I was choking to death. "Let's go to a fun bar and—"

But I told her I'd throw up at the sight of a meal, and the faster we got a present for my mother, the faster we'd get home. In about three minutes she was in a ski store with the perfect present—a black designer one-piece ski suit. I was so excited. I wasn't sure Mom would ever be able to ski again (since she'd broken her shoulder three times and then her ankle and she had a bad knee and she was "too old," according to my father), but the ski suit would give her hope.

Every year, Mom and Dad went out to dinner and church on Christmas Eve with really good friends. It distracted them. The first Christmas after Timmy died that August, and Alex had vanished like a ghost, my parents and I spent Christmas Eve and Christmas Day alone. It was the worst experience any of us had ever been through, I am certain. It was like we were holding our breath under water just to get through it.

Tina and I picked up the kids from my parents and brought them home for Christmas Eve. I missed being able to read "Twas the Night Before Christmas," but Kerry would have had a fit. We cooked steaks and baked potatoes, and made salad with blue cheese dressing, which were known at our house as the ultimate comfort foods. I told the kids Paul was doing Christmas things at Alex's, and since Alex had always been a part of their Christmas, they didn't seem upset. They pictured their father putting together dollhouses and bicycles, which hopefully he was doing. I simply had to trust that he was. And then, right before dinner, he called. I took it upstairs while Tina told the kids ghost stories.

While on the phone, I pretended I was on a cloud off a Caribbean island so that I would appear detached. It helped, actually. We went over the gifts for each child. We had agreed to make the Disney trip a big, wonderful, secret Christmas present. He wanted to take back the bike and dollhouse, but I told him no way. He was concerned about when I would pay him back my share. Finally, Paul promised he'd put together Jamie's bike and Kerry's dollhouse, but I knew he'd get Patrice or someone else to do it, since the guy couldn't even change the toilet paper roll.

It was Christmas Eve, after all, so Tina and I filled champagne glasses with ginger ale for the kids and toasted Christmas Eve. We made a toast to love and one to family and one to each of them.

"And to Daddy!" chimed Kerry. So, we made one to Paul.

"And to Patrice!" she continued, loving toasts. So, we made one to Patrice.

I finally got the kids to sleep. It was an ordeal, of course, because they were so excited, but it also was fun. Kerry insisted on making cookies and putting them outside for Santa so he wouldn't have hurt feelings. She wanted to draw a map to my parents' house, but I pointed out that Santa had been doing this for many years. Jamie was getting a little sick of it, since he knew there wasn't a Santa and the tree looked pretty sad with no presents underneath. I whispered to him that if this went on one more year, we'd just sit Kerry down and tell her Santa didn't exist at all.

"Screw Paul and Patrice." Tina and I were sitting on the back porch in our overcoats. We could see our breath, so I pretended I was smoking.

"Fuck them," I said again.

"I'm sure they're doing plenty of that," Tina replied.

The rain refused to turn to snow. I didn't care. I was outside, Tina was with me, Jackie was on my lap, the kids were asleep, and it was Christmas Eve. I looked up. "Happy birthday," I told Christ silently, like a prayer. "I need a little help, so when all this is over and you're not so busy I'd like to have a little chat."

"I just wonder what it will be like. Being single."

"It's like a candy shop," Tina explained.

I smiled. "Really?"

"All shapes and sizes." She paused. "That's incredible! You've never dated anyone but Paul, have you?" I was silent. "That's the scariest thing you've ever told me." She tipped her glass of champagne toward mine. "Watch out, world," she said. Tina always knew how to make me smile.

Sleeping wasn't easy. Tina was asleep beside me because she'd slept in Patrice's old room the night before and complained that it felt haunted, and since Paul and I had a king-size bed, so he could be as far away from me as possible, she slept in my room. I'd never seen anyone wiggle so much in my life. She was more active asleep than awake. My mother had demanded that we arrive at her house at seven-thirty "at the latest," which was a ridiculous request, but Jamie and Kerry usually woke us up at five on Christmas Day so it was fine. I had to look gorgeous and flirt heavily with Alex so Paul would be miserable.

Then I thought it was ridiculous to waste time on it. But then there was the pride factor. Finally, I convinced myself that it didn't really matter anymore.

I closed my eyes and tried to pray. After all, it was Christmas Eve night, a holy night, and certainly not one where a person should ask for anything. One should only be grateful. I ignored this. "God, I just need a little reassurance. I think something major's not going as planned."

"Eat your goddamn eggs!" Mom shrieked at Dad over our Christmas breakfast. The table looked perfect. A white-laced tablecloth covered the dining room table and crystal water glasses glistened under the chandelier. The sterling silver serving platters and casserole dishes, each with large silver serving spoons, were lined up at Mom's right so that she could serve. She'd made bacon, sausage, hash browns, eggs benedict with homemade hollandaise, freshly squeezed orange juice, coffee, and mimosas. And Dad had the nerve to be fiddling with his car radio when she called the family for breakfast.

After Mom's rampage, we ate in silence. No one wanted to risk saying anything annoying.

Mom sighed. "Carly, I just wish you'd gotten here a little earlier so we could have more time."

"We got here exactly at seven-thirty! I had to wake the kids up!"

"The day's half over," she announced.

It was eight-fifteen.

My parents had a torturous tradition of mandatory breakfast before presents were opened. I had seated Paul beside Mom because I thought he should be tortured more. Tina was on his other side, then Dad, then me, Kerry, Jamie, Alex, and Mom again. Paul and I had agreed not to tell my parents anything on Christmas Day. I was afraid Mom might slice him up with a carving knife. Dad would probably just get up and wander off somewhere. He hated confrontations.

"Great breakfast, Mama Cat," Jamie told her. The love. Her name was Catherine. Dad had always called her Cat. Jamie heard her being called either Cat or Mom, so he named her Mama Cat.

Mom's face softened and widened into a smile. "Thank you, lamb bone. I can't wait to see what you got for Christmas. It's so exciting! Everyone eat really fast so we can see what Jamie and Kerry got for Christmas!" Jamie loved that, of course.

"But," she stopped, "have you been good?"

"I've been really good," Kerry answered. "Jamie's very bad."

"I'm perfect!"

"Patrice says you're sloppy, like Mommy," Kerry countered.

Paul looked as if he'd been put in a straight jacket. He wouldn't glance left or right. He just stared straight ahead at the wall. His upper brow crinkled, which I knew meant he was nervous or upset. For a brief moment, I wanted to reach out my hand.

"Patrice says you're snobby, like Mommy." Jamie loved an audience.

"She did not." Kerry shook her head. "Well, she could have."

"Mommy's right here, remember?" I said, rebuffing them before this criticism fest went too far.

Kerry was out of her seat and on my lap. "I don't care that you're sloppy," she whispered, cupping her tiny hands around my ear.

Jamie mouthed "sorry" across the table.

"Mommy has such a pretty face," announced Kerry, stroking my cheek.

Don't do that, I'll start to cry, I thought. I needed to count to ten and visualize lying on a beach, the technique I had learned last week, when I still had a husband and a nanny.

"Carly, why are you breathing like that?" Dad asked.

Dad, who never notices anything? Paul could be gone ten years and he wouldn't realize it. I don't know where Dad lives in his mind, but I'd like to go there.

"You were counting backwards or something," Mom said.

"Oh God! I almost forgot my bloodies!" Tina announced. She leapt up, startling everyone, and marched into the kitchen.

"Oh, fantastic!" Mom was excited now. "You make the absolute best, I remember."

Tina came back with the bloodies. Everyone else was still watching me.

"Marry a handsome man and it's trouble," Dad announced lightly, from left field. Everyone looked around.

"I think *you're* handsome, Dad," I told him.

He grinned. "I'm the exception," he explained.

Everyone was quiet.

"Can…we…go…yet?" asked Kerry tentatively.

"Yes!"

Everyone jumped up and filed into the flawless living room. Alex lingered with me as I pulled myself together for a moment.

"It's taking everything in me not to slug him," I said.

"Luckily your mom doesn't know yet or he'd be dead by now." He smiled and put his arm lightly around my shoulder and led me into the living room.

Mom and Dad's house was cozy, elegant, clean, and beautiful without any apparent effort. I couldn't have prepared those meals or created this setting if I had fifty people to help me.

Dad put on "Joy to The World" and Mom lit the electric fire. I noticed Paul's moment of discomfort was gone. Here he was, having just left me to fuck the nanny, drinking my best friend's Bloody Mary's, eating my mom's eggs, attempting to joke with Alex, and taking all the credit for Jamie and Kerry's presents. I wanted to strangle him, but that would make everyone nervous.

We opened presents for hours, kids first. Mom used the same stockings that had been Timmy's and mine when we were kids. I wondered if that was hard for her.

After the stockings, they dove into the real thing. Jamie opened his presents in thirty seconds. Kerry unwrapped each one as if she were defusing a bomb. But they were very gracious, hugging and thanking the giver after every present.

Mom adored her ski suit and insisted on wearing it the rest of the day. After Dad opened his forty or so presents, he gave Mom a gift certificate. Mom had asked for a gold "I love you" bracelet. That's all she wanted. Dad seemed proud of himself and announced how great this present was because now his beloved wife could get whatever she chose for Christmas.

Mom glanced over at me and, luckily, she started to laugh. Then she got up and went over to give him a kiss. A few minutes later, she whispered to me, "Next year it's going to be different." I swear to God, the man had seen his last present.

Tina gave me a sloppy, sentimental goodbye kiss when we all left to change for dinner. "Just remember, anyone who is anyone loves you to pieces," she said.

I thought that was an odd analogy, since I felt I was already in pieces. "I'll be fine. I'm seeing you in three hours." And I gave her a hug.

I took the kids home and they both fell asleep in the living room. I went down to the basement and found all their summer clothes labeled and put away by Patrice. I packed sweaters and long pants for them as well, since Florida could be cold in December. My heart felt cold, that's for sure.

Paul arrived at 4:30 p.m. to watch Jamie and Kerry so I could go back to my parents' for Christmas dinner. Mom absolutely insisted on preparing the elaborate breakfast and dinner without help from any of us. It seemed a great way to ensure that she was the parent and Tina, Alex, and I were still children.

Paul's face looked blotchy-red and rough, his eyes were bloodshot, and his hands were shaky when he entered the kitchen, looking slightly bewildered and confused. Too many drinks, or maybe regrets? He immediately began pacing around, almost as if he had never been in his own house before. "That was the hardest morning. God, I feel awful about it. I mean, sitting there with your *parents...*" Paul stopped. "I fucked everything up," he announced.

I felt a tug of love for him. He looked so vulnerable.

That feeling was short-lived.

"What did your parents say after I left?" he wanted to know.

"Why do you care?"

He opened the icebox and grabbed a beer. "You're right. They're your parents so they'll believe whatever you tell them." He looked relieved. "So I don't really care."

"I was thinking of chopping off your head."

Paul didn't seem to hear me because he was concentrating deeply on the most important thing in his life: himself. "I feel much better. I'm very excited about the trip," he confided.

"Tell the kids about Disney when I'm gone," I said. "Don't let them sleep forever." And I left as fast as I could.

I slipped into the kitchen when I got back to my parents' house. Mom was threatening the creamed onions. "You assholes! If you curdle on me, I'll—"

"Catherine! It's Christmas, for God's sake!" Dad admonished her.

Then get up and help, I wanted to say. I entered the kitchen just in time for the meltdown—the missing carving knife, overcooked sweet potatoes, miscalculated turkey-cooking time...but the creamed onions were sending Mom over the edge. "Fuckers," she hissed at them so Dad wouldn't hear.

Alex wore a gorgeous pinstripe suit. Nothing like a man dressed to the nines to make a woman forget her troubles. Take me now! I wanted to say. Tina arrived in a black dress so short I thought it was a shirt. Dad loved it, though. Mom looked ravishing with all her jewelry and elegance. I ran upstairs, put on her make-up, and borrowed a velvet dress. There.

The dinner turned out beautifully. My mother always pulled it together in the end. Everyone drank champagne, and we were all giddy and toasting and glowing when Dad announced he had a little surprise. He grabbed his glass and the bottle of champagne and insisted we all follow him into the living room where he popped in a video of people skiing with no legs. At least that's what it looked like at first. Actually, they physically *had* legs, they just didn't work—their knees or ankles were debilitated or missing. Then Dad held up a strange metal contraption.

"What is this?" Mom demanded.

"It's a way to ski if you're disabled. It cost five hundred dollars! Merry Christmas to my beautiful bride." He held up his glass in triumph.

Dad then brought out this gigantic box from his bathroom and in it was a seat that was supposed to attach to the back of Mom's thighs and skis. With this miraculous invention, Dad explained, Mom could float down the mountain like a bird without putting any weight on her fake knee and old, decrepit legs. Dad was beaming.

We must have played that video fifty times trying to follow the directions and get Mom strapped in properly. By that time she was exhausted and asked for more champagne. Then she checked herself out in the living room mirror.

"I look like a bloody idiot," she hissed at Alex, Tina, and me when Dad was in the bathroom. "And who's going to get me into this contraption every time?" She seemed more interested when Alex said he would.

But none of us could see how it would work on the slopes without taking the video on the chair lift. Mom stood there looking hysterically funny, Dad was onto other things and was struggling with a radio remote control for his bathroom, and Tina, Alex, and I were laughing so hard that it took us just as long to get Mom free as it had to get her strapped in.

For a while, I was almost fine.

SEVEN

The kids seemed confused and excited about Christmas and the sudden trip to Disney World. They hadn't had time to fully grasp that I wasn't going. Paul pulled up in a stretch limo at 7:00 a.m. all dressed for Florida, the hair on his toothpick pale legs bristling when they hit the cold air. (Patrice was meeting them at the airport. Smart chick.)

As Jamie climbed in, he turned to me. "Come down and surprise us if you can, Mom. We'll really miss you." He looked at me solemnly. "No one else will go on the Supersonic Slide." I held him so tight I thought he'd protest.

Kerry gave me a hug and whispered, "I bet you did this for us!" And the look in her eyes was so wise that I felt she had a thousand-year-old soul in that tiny body. Because, in a way, I *had* done it for them.

"Hey, can I have the BMW while you're gone?" I asked Paul, who was standing by the front seat watching me. He walked over to me.

"No." And he gave me a hug and a kiss on the cheek and they were gone. I walked around the yard thinking about so many things that, before I realized it, an hour had passed. This particular habit drove Paul crazy. He hated, for example, when I went to pick up the laundry and then I forgot it at the cleaners. He got slightly testy if I went to buy groceries and ended up at a bookstore. Or if I made an attempt to be the dutiful housewife and ironed the sheets, got bored and left, and burned them all up. This distressed him.

I walked up the driveway and stopped to stare at the house. It wasn't a terrible house, although it was more like a cottage. The ceilings were low and everything in it was old, but this gave it "charm." I thought it would be nice to live in a house where things actually worked.

The exception was the kitchen. I actually did burn down the old kitchen by accident, and the insurance got me a new one. The sheets were a blip on the radar screen compared to that fiasco. I had simply placed the toaster innocently underneath the paper towels, forgetting that the toaster was old and broken and if you didn't physically remember to pop the toast up, it would just keep going. I put in some English muffins and went to take a quick shower and became entranced with this new hair dye that said in big letters (nothing is in big letters on shampoo bottles anymore, which is insane since it is impossible to read in a hot shower under normal conditions, so if you need glasses it's a joke) you could only keep this dye on "for exactly two minutes, not a second more." I took this seriously, since my thick hair was my best suit and I didn't want it all to fall off in piles like I had cancer as I combed through it after the shower.

I was concentrating extremely hard on making this all work perfectly with a stopwatch and everything, vaguely aware of an alarm of some kind, when three firemen burst into my bathroom and grabbed me out of the shower stark naked, covered (not wrapped, covered) me with a towel as I fought them off, desperately trying to explain that I had thirty seconds to wash out the dye so I couldn't go anywhere. They scooped me up and carried me out the door and plopped me on the driveway in this wet towel while they fought the flames shooting out of the roof and windows of the kitchen. There was snow on the ground, a rarity in Washington, but it was February and extremely cold. I crept over to an unused fire hose and quickly turned it on my hair, but it was so strong it knocked me right down. It practically sprayed my hair right off the top of my head, but I was pretty sure I got the dye out.

I didn't have to cook for four months, my hair looked gorgeous, I had a state-of-the-art new kitchen, and I suppose I was lucky Paul didn't divorce me right then. He must have really loved me after all.

I wasn't going to miss Paul one bit, I decided now, trying desperately to block out the image of him sweeping my children away to fantasy land, trying to block out the loss of a dream, of my life, of all I wanted, of the reality that we were acting *separated,* terrifying reality that kept slapping at my mind, making me pay attention—*it's over, life as you know it is gone*—the hurt that was too much to digest, the little girl inside with no place to go, the crushing helplessness, humiliation, hurt, inevitability, and aloneness of it all.

I was still outside in the driveway, reluctant to enter the empty house. I realized it was the very first time I'd be living there all alone and I marched in like a drill sergeant thinking this would be an excellent time to retain my rights as mistress of the house and thus began briskly cleaning up the kitchen.

I looked around and it hit me: I was really going to miss Patrice. Patrice kept the spoons together in the drawer. She went to the grocery store with actual lists and then cooked food and cleaned it all up afterwards. She even folded the sheets and put them in little piles with the right pillowcases. She waited for repairmen—lots and lots of repairmen, thousands of them— and I knew she loved me. I had really believed she did. She had taken away days of endless chores followed by the dread of Paul's arrival home with his critical eye ready to devour me. More and more, Carly had disappeared under a napkin.

Paul got jealous, I thought. He did it on purpose. "Of all the girls in the world," I told Jackie dramatically, ad-libbing "Casablanca."

This was good. I had to hate Paul with as much energy as possible, thereby delaying any pain. I could deal with pain gradually. Good plan.

I turned on every light in the house. Then I took my wedding ring off and had a little farewell ceremony. I packed away all of Paul's clothes and put them in the garage. I took down every picture that had him in it and cut him out. The whole process was exhausting, so I decided I deserved to go buy myself some belated Christmas presents to cheer me up. Of course, I hadn't gotten a present from Paul. If he had bought one, he probably gave it to Patrice. I thought I could buy a few little things that would make me feel better: twelve lacy panties, eleven pairs of stockings, ten brand new nails, nine juicy books, eight kinds of lotion, seven bottles of wine, six packs of cigarettes, four wild lipsticks, three pairs of earrings, two take-out dinners, and five golden rings…

I was kind of singing in a cheerful refrain, resembling a deranged murderess filling the courtroom with her defiant voice as she was led off to life in prison. Jackie looked worried. I was a little worried, I told Jackie. Then the phone rang.

"Hi, doll. I absolutely can't stand this house one more second. I'm so bored. I'm going to run away from home. Your father stopped drinking for a whole month. If you thought he was tedious before, you can't even *imagine* …and you know how I hate the day after Christmas, and you must be so lonely there all by yourself! I bet you could just die in a pile." She took a breath. "Please come over?"

I found it distressing to look at my caller ID and realize the only calls were from my mother. I laughed. I was there in 10.

"Anyway, you, gorgeous Carly Russell (what about Macalister? I wondered), are young with a huge future ahead. I know about that slimy husband of yours. I wanted to take a contract out on him, but I wasn't sure who to contact."

I just sat there. Mom always knew everything. I found it annoying.

"Tina! When did she tell you? I know it was her," I hissed.

"Oh, darling, it was Alex." Mom leaned forward, "Can you believe he gave us a trip to Paris? Your father will never go, so it's you and I. If you fall in love with someone French that would be the ultimate irony, right?" I smiled, trying to keep up. "So, anyway, I've had plenty of time to plan my revenge, but I can't have Paul killed because he's my grandchildren's father."

"A sticky situation," I agreed.

"I think you're going to have a grand new life. Paul (she made a face when she said his name) admittedly was very cute when you met him. But he had a mean streak. He doesn't respect women. He was always bad for you, Carly. He stole the life right out of you." She picked up her glass and raised it to me. "You should be dancing in the streets thanking God you are free of him."

Well, that was certainly an optimistic way to look at things.

Mom doesn't like to waste time. She had already made a list of potential suitors for me. She knew a friend whose nephew had just moved to town. He was forty-two and very successful. And the other day on the metro she had sat next to an adorable man who was a teacher at a school close by. She had his card somewhere. And then there was that lobbyist she met at a party last week. He was so cute.

I tried to imagine it. "Hi, my husband of fifteen years just left me for my nanny, but hey, sure, I'm ready to date."

"Mom, can't we just wait a little while?"

"All the good ones get snatched up," she sighed. "But I guess a few days would be okay."

That night, Paul called from Florida. Yes, the kids were fine, trip was easy, yes, it's sunny and gorgeous, but the reason for the call was to tell me that I needed to see a shrink.

"I'm hanging up on you," I warned him.

"You're going to hang up on me so you don't lose your temper, right?"

"I have good reason to lose my temper. You've ruined my life."

Paul had actually made an appointment with this psychologist. He said my family was abnormal. I told him *his* was abnormal. I mean, even if it were slightly true (about my family), what business was it of his? But he wouldn't let it go.

"Carly, you have to face it: you're disorganized, irritable, and slightly manic."

"Paul, you're selfish, a cheater, a lousy parent, and a liar."

"You need therapy," Paul continued.

"You didn't hear a word I said." I never even knew he knew the word "therapy."

"His name is Dr. Knot and your appointment is tomorrow at noon."

"His name is *not* Dr. Knot!"

"The tying kind," he explained.

"But *still.*"

"My treat. 1642 Connecticut Avenue. Walking distance."

"No chance in hell. *You* go to the damn shrink."

At noon the next day I had my first meeting with Dr. Knot. I called Tina and told her about it, expecting her to roar with laughter or express her indignation that Paul would ever suggest such a thing, but instead she volunteered to do all my errands so I wouldn't have an excuse not to go. I was grateful, but also slightly irritated. Like I was the only one who needed a little help? She had orange and purple hair. And she was short.

The shrink's receptionist, Liza, handed me a novel to fill out while I waited. I agonized over the questions. Question 12: Do you drink?

"But of course, don't you?" I wanted to ask the questionnaire back.

Question 17: Have you ever felt depressed?

"Well, yes, haven't you? You're just a questionnaire! How pathetic is that? I'd be depressed if I were you. And you're nosy as well. This is my private life. I don't even know you."

Liza noticed I was talking to myself and gently told me the doctor was ready to see me. Then she ushered me into his office and closed the door. The Knot was kind of stocky in a cute kind of way, with thick salt-and-pepper hair and large black eyes that looked huge behind his glasses.

"Is there any particular place you'd like me to sit?" I asked. The chairs, tables, floor, and sofa were strewn with papers. I loved that. It made me feel at home.

"Anywhere's fine," he responded kindly.

Okay, I liked him. Paul would not know this, ever, I swore to myself right there.

I moved some magazine articles and sat down on a leather couch and he came around from his desk and sat facing me in a matching leather chair.

"So, are you here because your husband insisted on it, or did you decide to keep the appointment on your own?"

Hmm. Interesting, tricky question in case Knot was a spy. Oh well, I'd sue him if he was for the doctor/patient confidentiality thing. So I got right down to the point. "I drive my husband crazy. This was a gene passed down from my mother."

"How do you drive him crazy?" He started writing things down on a lined yellow pad.

"He thinks I'm an impatient, angry, frigid, disorganized bitch," I explained.

The Knot pondered this. "You're not a bitch."

I burst out laughing. The hour went so fast I almost challenged him when he told me time was up.

The rest of the week went by really fast and it was kind of fun, being so free. No husband! No kids! Other times it was no fun at all. I cried a lot, come to think of it. It was a horrible week.

EIGHT

Alex looked quite dashing in his camel overcoat and black leather gloves the night I met him at Austin Grill for dinner. We sat down opposite each other and I pretended I belonged to him.

"You look lonely," Alex commented. "But très chic."

"Don't talk French to me," I snapped. I was wearing something untypical for the Austin Grill, where blue jeans were just fine. I didn't care. My black tights and high-collared black knit dress with platform shoes made me feel like I could be tall and powerful, which of course was not how I felt at all.

Alex reached over and felt my arm. "It doesn't drip."

"Men think women's arms drip?"

"Big turn-off. You know, when it's all white and jiggly under here." He felt the underside of my arms, which I instinctively tensed to be taut. "See how firm those are?"

One of us was clearly having an out-of-body experience.

"Are you that desperate for conversation?" I asked him, nearly too loudly, close to over-the-top, like I needed to say, "Calm down, Carly! Everything is normal here."

The crabmeat enchiladas, shrimp soft tacos, and corn soup arrived and I couldn't touch any of it, although it was my favorite food on earth. It would be my last meal if I ever got executed. "I can't believe you never get lonely," I told Alex in a hushed tone, tearing up my napkin and twirling the pieces into long sticks and then lighting a match to them. Alex once told me that he's never, ever felt lonely. How could that be, I had always wondered. Maybe, by nature, men didn't feel the need to be close to someone the way women did. The other possibility was that I was very needy and immature.

Alex leaned forward and held my hand. I pulled it away. "Carly, the only way to get over this *thing* you're going through is to meet someone hot and forget that asshole you married! And that means you have to go on dates."

Dating's like golf. Just when you're going to give it up completely, you have one great outing and you're hooked again. Basically, however, it's a frustrating, futile, expensive, time-consuming, humiliating experience...just like golf.

"You don't even need to *like* the person," Alex assured me.

A customer of mine entered the restaurant—the one who was making my life at work hell and the one who sentenced me to that horrid seminar. Maria Slovinski was peering around the room like a rat. I once told Ellie that God was on acid when he made this woman. Ellie almost sent me to another seminar.

"Oh, shit, I'm going to die." I tried to look down.

Slovinski had money but she reeked of envy, like a person who couldn't be filled up no matter how big her house was or how often she went to church. Because when she went to church, she'd look around to see who else was there. How could you feel full if you were a person like that?

I peered up, craving danger, and she onto me. "Carly, darling. How convenient. I'm just meeting my lawyer for dinner." She turned her head and stared at Alex like she was eying a steak. "Well, what have we here? Carly, you always have the most attractive men."

Alex stood up, of course. She put out a limp hand, like she expected Alex to kiss it, "I'm Maria Smith." Then, she maneuvered herself right past him and plopped down in the booth. She patted for him to sit. "And you are?"

Poor Alex looked around and reluctantly sat back down next to her. "Alex Dunn," he replied, barely acknowledging her.

"Sit down, John," she told her lawyer, slightly annoyed he hadn't followed suit.

He hesitated. "Perhaps this isn't the best time."

Someone has manners, I thought. And someone has the sexiest voice, shoulders, eyes, hair, and body that I'd seen in, say, twenty years.

"Oh, they'd love it, wouldn't you, Carly?"

Everyone waited.

Hmm. Yes, fine, John, sit right down, baby. I said nothing.

"John, please sit down?" Maria's voice sounded desperately casual—a little wobbly like, "Get your ass down or I'll fire you."

"It's just more festive this way, all of us together, don't you think?"

Sit! I thought. I wanted to touch him. He made me horny. Or the second margarita was. I kind of giggled. The situation was so absurd. John was beside me, obeying his client, and he and I started having a private conversation without saying a word. A reach for the water...a brush of an elbow...a quick side glance...

Luckily Maria, with a voice like a sick cat, was demanding that Alex tell her everything about doctors, and the words between John and I floated between us. They were actually half-whispers.

"Why were you laughing?" he asked, his thigh finding mine.

"Don't play dumb, Counselor. It's just funny." I gave him a Lady Di look. God, I wanted to fuck him.

"It's humiliating." His tongue flicked my ear.

"Representing her? Typical lawyer. Guess you'd do anything for money."

"Horrid thing to say. Are your eyes green or blue?"

"If you represent Slovinski, you don't deserve to know."

His drink came. I slurped up my second and he sipped his first.

"She hired the firm. I'm an innocent employee," John explained.

"You don't look innocent." We looked each other up and down. I put my mouth to his ear, "My place or yours?" And we both burst out laughing.

Maria glanced up with a quick frown.

So we spoke without moving our lips.

"Do you have a last name, John?" I asked, "You know *my* name, of course, since you're suing me."

"Davenport. Is that your boyfriend?"

"One of them. Just tell me how you plan to get her out of it?" I loved his teeth. Actually, his entire mouth. Those shoulders. Those eyes. He looked me up and down, the flirt. He should have been ashamed, the way he was looking at me.

"Damn. And I thought you were the kind of woman who likes surprises."

I shrugged. "Fine. Let's make a bet who wins." He smiled and we clinked glasses without them touching. "Because I will. Just so you know," I added.

"You," he said, our faces so close we were practically kissing, "think of the terms."

"Carly, where is that philandering husband of yours off to this time?" Maria's voice snapped at me like a rattlesnake.

"I'm still married, Slovinski. Macalister's fine."

How could you represent her?

Maria's specially made drink arrived. She thought it was too sweet. "More gold in this one," she called to the waiter, flicking her finger at him.

"Please," I corrected her. "May I have some more gold tequila, please?"

Alex gave me a warning look.

I excused myself and went to the ladies room to try to get a grip and to check my make-up. I looked totally gorgeous! How convenient. I practiced making seductive gestures in front of the mirror. I practiced mouthing my words, a demure smile, and a toss of the hair. The thought did cross my mind that I hadn't touched a morsel of dinner, and Austin Grill was famous for making the strongest, most delicious margaritas in D.C., and then I realized I was playing in dangerous waters that could cost me forty thousand dollars and destroy my reputation all for a fuck. I walked back to the table carefully.

Slovinski ignored me and continued monopolizing the conversation when John and Alex rose as I sat down. "Now, you don't think a single girl should be forced to buy a house if she doesn't want to, do you?" Maria asked Alex, touching his arm, her voice Kool-aid girlish, making my skin crawl. I just come out to have a nice, calm dinner with Alex and she invades our table like a cockroach, with the nerve to try to win over my best friend right in front of me?

"I don't think this is the time to—" John tried, but Slovinski kept right on talking to Alex.

"It's nothing against Carly, except she should have explained to me that I absolutely had to have an inspection or else I could never ask for anything to be fixed, and, well, I'm just so nervous that something might be wrong. I didn't know the rules. You see?"

"I think we should refrain from this con—" John had his hands up.

"Didn't know the rules?" I hissed at her. "That you had a right to an inspection? I only told you every day and finally warned you six times in writing to hire one!"

"The house hasn't gone to settlement. Therefore, I have the right to back out of the contract." If she touched Alex again I'd claw her to death.

"If you don't come to settlement, you'll lose your entire deposit." My voice was gritty.

"Let's discuss this at the appropriate time," John announced firmly.

Maria ignored him too. "Carly, if you need the money from the commission, if that's it, I could help you perhaps."

"You're just a spoiled little bitch."

I probably should have nibbled on some salsa and chips before my second drink.

"What's this?" asked John, trying to diffuse the situation.

"I was burning up napkins," I explained.

Slovinski's face was growing into a red balloon. "Apologize," she demanded of me, rising dramatically. "I want you to. NOW!"

"Sorry, Slovinski." To John, "Nice date. Do you bring her out often?"

"That's not good enough." Maria's voice stopped the room. Her upper lip was trembling. I was having fun in a sick way, realizing the value of *not* losing your temper.

"John, control your animal, would you?" I asked John softly, touching his arm.

That was it. She slammed her drink on the floor and it smashed into pieces. She looked like she was going for my neck when John and Alex both leapt up and held her arms, talking quietly, trying to calm her, apologizing to the other customers, while she flailed her arms to get free in her overstuffed Gucci jacket.

I just smiled sweetly at her and mouthed, "No taste," which made her even more furious, and John was forced to throw a fifty on the table and escort her out of the restaurant. Like a bouncer. A minute later he was back, leaning over and kissing me on the cheek goodbye—his tongue lingering on my skin and his breath in my ear.

"I'm calling off the bet," he whispered. "Too risky."

I laughed and we smiled at each other. I was in love. He shook Alex's hand, apologized to both of us for Slovinski's behavior, and he was gone.

"There must be an easier way to be treated to dinner," I told Alex.

"You are a vixen. You're definitely going to court."

"That was fun. Did you see her face?" I was all worked up.

"Fun? Maybe we need to get you out more often."

Outside the restaurant, Alex took my arm. "I think you had a crush on that guy. You were all flushed. I could tell."

I broke away. "Where the hell is my car? Damn." I looked all around.

"You always park behind. I'll drive you to it. Are you okay?"

"How do I look? Did I look good in the restaurant? How's my hair?" John had only seen me from the side most of the time. "Look at my profile." I turned my head.

"Carly, Maria Slovinski is his client. He's your enemy. You're acting insane." We reached his car and Alex let me in. I needed to kiss someone.

"I feel like kissing you. Do you mind?"

"One drink next time. Yes, I mind, because you'll hate me tomorrow."

"How do you know?" I put my hand on his thigh. He took it off.

"Because you're not in love with me and you know it."

"Fine, I'll go out with John then."

"That's a grand idea. Now, where's your car?" But he reached closer and kissed me lightly on the mouth, his blazer grazing my arm, and his fingers lightly intertwined with mine. "You're like an accident waiting to happen," he told me.

I had heard that before.

NINE

New Year's Eve would have been perfectly fine if it hadn't been for my mother. My week had been peaceful. The house was actually being nice to me. Nothing major had broken. I tried to explain to her that it wasn't that big a deal to me, that Paul and I never did anything special for New Years, anyway, and I really wasn't upset about spending one quiet evening alone. What about the next 364? I wanted to ask her. What about the next fifty years?

She left messages all afternoon:

3:00 p.m. "Hi, doll. It's your mother calling. God, I bet you're absolutely thrilled this year is finally over! Next year is going to be your best ever," she continued. "Your father and I have already discussed it, and we are both sure. So don't you dare get down. Just wondering if you have any plans yet for tonight. Give me a ring."

3:30 p.m. "Carly? It's Mother. What about that horrid mortgage guy? He's not much, but I bet he'd give his right arm to take you to dinner tonight. I think you should call him right up. Pretend your real date got in a car accident or something."

4:00 p.m. "Hi, dear, it's your mother. I also was thinking of that lawyer. I know he's an alcoholic, but no one's perfect. Besides, lawyers can come in very handy. Why don't you just give him a quick call? Maybe you could pretend you're involved in a lawsuit and need advice."

5:30 p.m. "Carly, Dad and I have decided you must come to the dance with us since..." Oh no. Quickly, I grabbed the phone.

"Hello? What?"

"Where have you been?" Mom demanded. "Are you not answering your phone again? I hate it when you do that."

"I went for a walk. A very, very long walk."

"Anyway, your father and I have decided there is no way we can have fun at the dance knowing you're home alone."

"Yes, you can, you've been doing it since I was six."

Silence. That wasn't very nice. Why did I say that? "Just kidding."

"You're coming with us," she announced.

"I am not!" I responded, a little too harshly. "I mean, I would love to, but really, I'll be perfectly fine. The kids are gone. It's peaceful. It's really great." Silence still. "Look, I really don't think I want to go out tonight."

"Okay, I understand that, but I certainly don't want you to be sad."

"I promise, Mother. Truly. I might even go to a party with Tina."

"Well, if you're invited, of course you're going!"

"Of course. Love you, Mom."

We hung up. Then Tina called.

"Why haven't you picked up your phone?" She sounded irritated.

"I thought you were my mother."

"So you don't answer the phone on New Year's Eve? Now that's a brilliant way to make sure you have absolutely nothing to do."

"As if I'd go out with anyone who called now." No one seemed to understand it was fine to stay home.

"My loser date and I are picking you up at seven-thirty," Tina told me.

"You don't know his name?"

"Jeff something. I don't know. Maybe I should cancel." She sounded confused.

"You haven't even met the guy. Maybe he's great."

"What great guy would go on a blind date on New Year's Eve?" she wanted to know. I couldn't answer that. "Please come with us."

We'd been arguing about this for days. Even Alex had a date. I tried not to think about that. It made me vaguely uneasy.

"What else are you going to do? Watch TV all night?"

"Of course not! I'm not that pathetic."

I just wish I hadn't sat and watched TV all night. The shows were horrid. I should have read a book. Reading a book demonstrates intellectual curiosity as well as an ability to truly enjoy being by oneself. TV demonstrates a desperate attempt to remain distracted. But I was extremely proud of myself that I had not **once**—of the hundred times I almost did—used star sixty-seven and called John's number to see if he was home or if a woman answered. I refrained. Of course John would have plans. I had only met him two days before and we were enemies in a court case, otherwise I knew I would be out with him. It was kind of fun to torture myself thinking about him all night since it definitely beat thinking about reality.

The night the kids got back everything went better than I expected, even as the three of us watched Paul (sun-burnt and puffy-faced) pay the limo driver and dump Kerry and Jamie's presents from his family and their luggage by the door. "Help us bring it all in, you lazy selfish shit," I thought. But I just remained above-it-all (due to instructions from the Knot) and watched him speed away in his basically untouched brand new BMW he bought himself as a surprise for his birthday.

Kerry, Jamie, and I dragged all their stuff up to their rooms. All their clothes were dirty, thanks Paul. You know how I love laundry. I'd bought them each new posters and new bedcovers, and you'd have thought they won the lottery, they were so excited. The icebox was full and, this seemed to be a huge hit. Then they spotted their new lunch boxes and jumped up and down hugging me. Next year for Christmas I'm giving them food, covers, and lunch boxes.

We had grilled cheese and tomato sandwiches in my bed and watched a Disney movie I rented and, once again, they were thrilled about this. It's like I'd never done anything for them before. Maybe they missed me. This thought made me cry.

"Oh no," Jamie said in a low voice. "Here it comes."

"Here what comes?" I demanded.

"Jamie's the man of the house," Kerry explained. "Daddy told him."

"And he said to expect lots of tears." This low, manly voice of Jamie's was alarming.

"Jamie, you don't have to take care of me. I take care of you, remember?" He shrugged. "I was crying because I love you."

He shook his head. "Whatever you say, woman," he replied like a little man. It sounded so absurd that we all started laughing.

"Call me Mom,, okay?"

"Okay, woman." And they were in hysterics again.

They did let it slide out that Patrice left the second day of their trip, disgusted with Paul for some reason young children aren't able to explain. Her departure would have had more of an impact on the kids if they hadn't been at Disney World with fourteen cousins, five uncles, two aunts, a grandma, and their father. But now that the kids were home, surely they would notice Patrice's absence due to our differing techniques regarding laundry, meals, organization, etc. This realization drove me into a complete panic.

I checked on them about six times before I went to bed just to make sure they were still there and hadn't sneaked back to their father. The last time I crept into their rooms it was two in the morning. I had spent the evening pacing around the house and making ridiculous lists and I knew it was time for bed when one of the pieces of paper just read, "Food." Of course I had gotten tons of food before they came home. I was totally prepared for a smooth transition into single-hood-with-no-help. Bed was definitely in order when you write that kind of list, so finally I went upstairs.

Jamie's a restless sleeper, like me, and he'd apparently been at war with his covers, which were knotted and wrapped tightly around his legs. He was still thrashing around a little, and he smiled, yawned, and mumbled, in that order, when I straightened everything out. Kerry sleeps so that her sheets and blankets don't even move. She could slip out of them in the morning and the bed would be made up. I gave her a kiss and pushed her corn-colored hair back so I could feel the softest, smoothest cheek in my world. She had "Liony," who only had one eye now and about half of his stuffing, clutched in her arms. She looked like a half-melted vanilla ice cream cone. And probably forever to come, the thought invaded my mind for the first time: I can see how he could leave me, but how could he leave them? Because no matter how close he lived, we weren't a family, so it wasn't the same.

It took me a week or so to understand that Patrice had vanished into thin air and then I went into meltdown mode.

It didn't matter that much about Paul, but I had held onto the belief that she'd definitely come back to me. And it certainly didn't help that the next few weeks were freezing, windy, cloudy, with frozen sleet falling almost every day so the roads were treacherous even without any snow. At least when it snowed you could go sledding. People moved around. It was magical out. There was nothing magical about freezing rain. There was nothing so great about a husband screwing around on you for an entire marriage and then leaving, either. And every time I thought of something funny, I'd think, "Oh, I can't wait to tell Patrice," before I remembered.

At least Paul whizzed in and out of our lives like a boomerang, taking the kids and occasionally giving me a break (I never admitted I needed one, of course), but it was hard never knowing when he was coming or going or if we were getting divorced or what he was up to. Frankly, it was all getting so depressing that I could barely get out of bed. I was convinced that some drastic disease had ravaged my body and I would be put in the hospital where Paul would come visit with tears, flowers, gifts, and beg for me to take him back.

Instead, when I explained this all to the Knot, he instructed me to write down my goals every day.

"You are not sick. You are depressed."

"Of course I'm depressed! I'm a single, old bat."

DAY ONE GOALS:

1 Get out of bed

2 Sue ex-husband

3 Find new man who is willing to do everything

4 Find Jamie another school (start fresh due to 8 missing library books)

5 Find stamps

6. Make edible dinner

I felt a little better, although the list for my first day looked slightly daunting. By noon, I had gotten out of bed and made hamburger meat into three flat circles.

"What kind of mother was your mother?" the Knot asked after I had given him my list. We saw each other a little more often than I had originally planned, like every day.

"My mother's inconsequential." I needed Patrice.

"Are you angry with your parents?"

"Not at all. I think they're cute."

The Knot definitely didn't have to know about their fake dog. My parents get notices from the Humane Society because of calls from nosy neighbors who believe Mom and Dad are harboring some poor animal that has never seen the light of day. Actually, the loud, ferocious bark is from one of Dad's gadgets, designed to keep burglars out, but sometimes it breaks and barks whenever it wants to. Dad loves gadgets. Mom said if he dropped dead tomorrow she'd never be able to watch TV again. You couldn't just turn it on. And Dad is so obsessed with the newest technology in all mechanical devices that my mother tells anyone who will listen that she could go to Europe for a month and Dad wouldn't notice except he'd have no dinner.

But Dad was distinguished in appearance and demeanor. "A man of few words— A man with integrity," he is often called. His hair was white and covered his head lightly, as though it could blow away like a dandelion.

"There's something more going on here." Knot's voice jolted me back to his office. "Have you ever asked yourself, 'Why do I have this empty feeling?' Usually it has something to do with childhood, you see."

"My parents are as normal as they could be." I was getting impatient. I wanted to talk about *me.*

"I'm having creepy house dreams," I offered. They were terrifying—*leaking roof, carpenter ants, faulty faucets, dry rot, dead plants, lawns to be mowed, laundry to be folded, food to be cooked…*

(I like romantic dreams better)

… Homework to be supervised, light bulbs to replace, bills to find, refrigerators to be cleaned, drawers to be lined…Car to be serviced, checkbook to balance, package to be mailed, thank you notes to be written…

But Knot told me he couldn't solve this problem immediately. "Just make lists and complete them. You'll feel better."

I tried another tactic, leaning forward. "Paul likes to humiliate me. He's trying to make me crazy."

He leaned forward as well. "Love and hate are very similar, you know."

"Thanks. Here's your ninety bucks."

TEN

Even though I still felt sick, everyone was convinced it was in my mind. I certainly didn't want the whole world to think I was insane, so I decided to take the kids after school and pretend that going to the grocery store would be *really fun*. I greeted them at the kitchen door freshly showered and made up in black Capri pants, platform shoes, and wearing a frozen, false smile just as Kerry and Jamie were about to enter (they had started taking the bus to school, which was a godsend) and scared them half to death.

"Hi, kids! Let's be normal and go to the store together!"

They stood there.

"Mom, you look weird." Jamie seemed concerned.

"Mommy-, you look like you were in a play." Kerry reached her hand up to my face. "Are you okay, Mummy?"

"Fine! Maybe I shouldn't have put on the red rouge." I backed up and they came into the kitchen, cautiously.

"I can't go to the store. I have a math test." Jamie peered in the refrigerator. "Jesus, Mom, couldn't you have gone to the store while we were at school? What do you do all day, anyway?"

"I haven't been feeling that well, Jamie. Come on, if we go together, you can get all the special things!" I ran to the bathroom to see why they were so horrified. I looked like a clown.

"Dad was right," I heard Jamie tell Kerry.

I marched out of the bathroom, "What does that mean?"

"He thinks you're crazy." Jamie's face was hot and red. "He thinks you're pathetic and you can't take care of us."

Kerry burst into tears, hit Jamie, and ran into me, hugging my waist. "Mummy's perfect!"

We went to the store.

I spent $238 on groceries and managed to unload them all, but I didn't actually put them away, because that seemed too tedious and I was feeling dizzy and I was hungry (which is always a drastic mistake, to go to the grocery store when you're hungry, because you buy everything in sight) I could not eat one thing in the grocery store because I had been caught doing this once, shoveling in some of those bulk-food yogurt-covered peanuts and looking like a chipmunk when some nosy, anal-retentive grocery clerk accosted me. I thought they were going to arrest me right then and there, but they let me go since it was my first offense and I was with two very concerned children.

So I was famished by the time I actually got home with the food—because I had been sick even though nobody believed me—and now I was really weak. I was sitting in the middle of the kitchen floor with all these snacks around me, eating a little bit of everything, and the kids were opening up all the boxes of cereal. I was feeling really happy no one would ever see me this way, when Alex knocked at the kitchen door. Unfortunately, we had a window in our kitchen door.

"WHY ARE YOU HERE?" I screamed through the door. This was definitely one of the most humiliating moments in my life.

He thought about this. "I missed you," he said through the glass. He looked around. "Are you okay?"

"Go away, right now!"

"Carly, let me in. You look terrible."

"I've been sick. I'm just a little hungry and tired." I looked around the kitchen floor but couldn't see the floor because all the groceries were covering it. "This is how I'm going to live from now on, so you better leave right now!"

Alex smiled. He always accepted me, even at my very worst.

"You don't have to be great in your own house; you're brilliant at work. Let me in. I'll help you," he persisted.

I wondered why Alex thought I was brilliant at work. He had overheard my phone calls, seen me running around with contracts or trying to find the address of a house I was supposed to be showing or searching frantically for the only key to one I had listed, so I didn't think I seemed particularly brilliant, but I was too weak to argue with him.

I let Alex in and he made me lie on the couch while he got the children started on their homework and put away the groceries. He cleaned the whole place up. The best part was, I really did have a high fever. Alex felt badly because he hadn't listened when I kept telling him how sick I felt, the Knot would owe me a thousand apologies, maybe I'd get to go to the hospital and make the party-boy ex actually take care of his children for once, and Jamie felt badly about what he said and it gave him hope that I might turn into a normal person eventually. I decided I was kind of a heroine, actually: going out into the cold, cruel world deathly ill in order to feed my starving children.

I heard Jamie calling his father in the kitchen. "Mom was sick the whole time. Maybe you could come over and do something for once." And he hung up. That wasn't exactly the ideal scenario; having a son so angry and confused he could barely function without screaming at one parent or the other. But it made me smile to myself, anyway. Dear, dear Jamie.

Alex made me tea and made the kids steak and baked potatoes. He brought me a cold cloth. Put on a video for the kids. He got me a blanket.

"If I had a nanny, I wouldn't be going crazy," I explained.

"We're getting you a housekeeper so you can go to work and be happy. You can't do all this and make money too. It's too much."

"Other people do it all the time." Then I remembered something. "Jamie has a huge math test..."

"I'll take care of it. Go to sleep. The kids will be fine."

He fed the kids, put me in bed, and slept on the couch. I almost said "I love you" in my weakened condition, but I've always been able to control myself emotionally so I didn't breathe a word.

A few weeks later, I was much better physically and had made huge strides on the emotional level as well. I only cried at the bank, at the gas station, at the gym, making dinner, watching television, reading, and talking on the phone. I cried at traffic lights, in the office, picking up the kids, at my parents, and at the Knot's. I sobbed and howled in the bathtub with the water going so the kids wouldn't hear.

I could not accept that Paul didn't miss me. How could anyone give me up like that? It was an outrage. I was special. It must be some cosmic mistake. He must be having huge regrets about all of this.

The deadline for any negotiation with Slovinski or her asshole lawyer, John, who still had refused to call and ask me to Aspen for the weekend or even out to dinner, had arrived. I had gotten the kids to school before my meeting with Ellie at the office with only four minor mishaps: Jamie admitted that he had a science project due that morning, which counted as one-third of his final grade, and he hadn't started it yet; the only bread had mold on it so I wasn't sure how to make lunch; Kerry got gum in her hair and screamed so loud when I tried to get it out I thought Protective Services would come any minute; and they missed the bus so we arrived at school twenty minutes late, which gave each of them a demerit.

I had just staggered in the door when my mother called. "Come over for breakfast, pumpkin, pretty please?"

"I can't. I've got to go to work."

"There's always something." I heard her sigh. I told her I'd call her back on the cell so I could put her on speaker and change from my robe to something more appropriate for work.

"I'm the ugliest, fattest, oldest-looking, scariest-looking creature that ever lived." This was how she answered the phone.

I should wear a suit. Then Ellie would think I was playing mommy/housewife and endangered realtor with ease. "Mom, you're not fat, you're a size eight," I called out to the bed where the phone was.

"Do you think they can amputate stomachs?" she asked. I could picture her standing sideways in front of her full-length bathroom mirror with the glaring, extra-bright, unrelenting lights, sticking out her stomach.

"Stop sticking your stomach out or it will stay that way permanently," I told her. "You look great. Promise. Have you put on your make-up yet?" I was struggling with the stockings.

"Christ, without my face on I'd scare the hell out of everyone."

"We all think you look wonderful, Mom, truly."

She was suddenly accusing. "You, how would you know? I haven't seen you in weeks!"

I started the car and put the cell down on the front seat. "I saw you yesterday." We have the same conversation all the time. I drove to work with an uneasy, guilty feeling, like I was the kind of daughter who would think nothing of dumping her mother in a seedy nursing home in Iowa and never seeing her again.

"It's the neck. How did it get like this?"

"The sun, Mom, remember? Just wear a turtleneck." Oops. The yellow light turned red at exactly the wrong time. I had to get her off the phone.

"And my eyes."

"Wear dark glasses."

"My arms droop."

"Wear long sleeves."

Finally I got to the office and she had to hang up, although she didn't seem happy about it at all.

"Carly Macalister, line one." My name was called out on the loudspeaker while I sat opposite my manager, Ellie, in her office, as she poured over (once again) Maria Slovinski's contract. The contract had every T crossed, so they could only get us on the lack of inspection, and the only proof I had was the word of the inspector I had called to do the inspection, who was in the hospital for a back operation and not in the mood to help me.

It didn't matter; Ellie was convinced Slovinski couldn't get out of settlement without losing her deposit. Ellie kept telling me that I had done nothing wrong.

"Go get your call," she ordered. She was a compact, brilliant workaholic who had compassion for nervous, inexperienced, disorganized agents like me, who happened to be blessed with the ability to sell.

"I don't want to. It'll either be my mother or John." John Davenport had been calling me all day. It would be different if he'd been calling me at home, asking me to come over and spend the night with him and have unbelievable sex. But the office?

"It's a man," added the receptionist, trying to be helpful.

"Answer it and see what he wants, Carly," Ellie told me. "We have to get this thing settled!"

I got up. "Did I tell you he was really cute?"

"Pretend he's a wolf," she advised.

I left her office and picked up the phone in the conference room. "Carly Macalister." It's hard to sound sexy and professional all at once.

"Mom?" It was Jamie.

"Yes. What is it?" I answered, irritated.

"The principal wants to talk to you." Oh shit.

"Why? Did you diss someone?"

"Gross!"

"Threaten a teacher, what?"

"I don't know! Honest." He sounded nervous.

"Carly Macalister, line two." The loudspeaker echoed through the office.

"Jamie, I have to take this.'

"Mom, it's the headmistress." His voice was pleading. "She says she needs to talk to you!"

"Carly Macalister, line two."

"Hold on, Jamie, I'll be right back." I pressed the hold button on line one and picked up two.

"Carly Macalister."

"Honey, that oaf just dumped me." It was Tina. She was sniffling and her voice was shaky. She was crying.

"Tina, I can't talk."

"Carly Macalister, line three."

"Of course you can! You're my best friend! I loved him."

"You just met him last week."

"Things were going so well."

"You slept with him, didn't you?"

"How did you know?"

"I have to call you back," I hissed.

"I'll hold."

"Fine." I pressed hold.

"Carly Mac…"

"Oh shut up, I know!" I yelled out to the reception room. I picked up line one. "Jamie. Tell her I've gone for the day."

"Mrs. Macalister?" It was the headmistress.

"Line three." Meek voice on the loudspeaker. Mental note: buy receptionist flowers.

"Hold on, please." I put her on hold. "Shit!" I pressed line three.

"What?" I screeched in the phone. There was a pause.

"Hello? This is John Davenport. Are you avoiding me?"

"No. I—"

"Are you all right?"

"Of course I'm all right. I just can't talk to you now."

"The settlement's tomorrow. When do you suppose you'll find the time?"

"Carly Macalister, you're son's principal is holding on line one. She says it's urgent."

"I have to go." Then, I thought, no, this is not good. "How about five this afternoon?"

"My office or yours?" I had to be home for Kerry when a neighbor (to whom I owed my life) dropped her off after ballet and Girl Scouts. "You'll have to come to my house. Kids. Five o'clock. Bye."

"Wait! The address!"

"Chevy Chase, D.C. Look it up." And I hung up. Back to line one.

"Mrs. Wheatly, I am so so sorry, I was having a minor catastrophe at work and I certainly would never encourage my child to lie about my whereabouts, but I was just leaving and—"

"Mrs. Macalister. Have you heard of attention deficit hyperactive disorder?"

I was in a hurry to get home and throw all the dishes and pans in the closet. That cute lawyer's coming to my house? And this pesky old woman/headmistress who probably hasn't been laid in a hundred years is bringing up this ADHD thing to me now?

"Oh please! Do not mention that over-used phrase to me. Of course I've heard of it, a little too much in fact, but Jamie is fine, and I think the whole concept is overstated because now apparently every child has ADD, and just because his papers are lost at home occasionally and I understand about the lost library books, and I know he never has an ironed uniform, I don't think—"

"I was talking about you." Then she went on to suggest that Jamie's organizational tutor be allowed to come see his room to check on the desk, lighting, and the presence of any "distractions." Gee, could she possibly mean the forty posters covering his walls, the comic books strewn all over the bed, the broken Nintendo, the stereo and speakers, CDs, telephone, six pair of tennis shoes...I couldn't believe it had gotten so bad. When Patrice was around, it had been perfect.

This nosy lady wanted to come over to my house? God!

"It's his tutoring day. Miss Donovan will be at your home at five o'clock. Jamie is slipping drastically in his studies and we need to get to the bottom of this."

"Today? Five o'clock today?"

I raced out of the office, forgetting that Tina was still holding for me on line two, and drove to Jamie's school to pick him up. I called Tina on my cell to apologize, but she was still on the other line waiting for me so I called my mother and told her to come over.

"You never let me in your house."

"Emergency."

Mom cleaned the kitchen in five minutes. Jamie and I filled up five garbage bags with stuff from his room and stashed them in the attic. But the room still looked like a disaster. It was hopeless. Right then, for once, Mom was brilliant.

"Just change rooms and make the guest room look like Jamie's, kind of like a movie set," she suggested.

"You mean, make the guest room Jamie's room for the day? What if we get caught?"

She ignored me. "We'll put a lamp on the desk, bring in a few pictures, throw some clothes in the closet, put his comforter over the bed, bribe Kerry, and lock his room. You should be fine."

"What about the lawyer?"

"Keep him in the kitchen." She looked me over. "You have fifteen minutes, Carly. And for God's sake, your nails look like claws."

She dragged me upstairs, fumbled through my closet, chose a gray jersey, lifted my arms up as if I were being arrested, tore off my shirt while I wriggled out of my skirt that I'd worn to work in order to look professional (but apparently my outfit was not up to my mother's standards), and then Mom threw the jersey over my head and pulled it down. She spat on my shoes and polished them with her fingers and scrambled around in the bathroom for nail polish.

"Hold still," she commanded, putting on a topcoat. "That'll do for now."

"Thanks, Mom."

"Offer him tea. Be professional. Here he comes."

It was too late for Mom to leave. I knew she was pleased with that. "I'll get it. Throw on a little blush, girl, you look like you just crawled out of a grave."

I heard her greet John and invite him into the kitchen. "Soo nice to meet you. My, are you handsome…Carly will be right down, she had quite a day. Jamie, will you say hello to? Ah, Mr. Davenport. Are you related to the Georgetown Davenports, by any chance? You're their son? Well, that's just fabulous! I went to your christening. I am not kidding. Your father had a crush on me in sixth grade. Yes, I grew up three streets down from your father. You're absolutely right. You must be, let's see, forty-one next month. Well, thank you, I've been told I have a fabulous memory. Did you go to St. Albans like your father? You did? Did you by chance know Timmy, my son? Yes? Well, thank you, we were proud of him too. Yes, he was quite the soccer player. You played lacrosse with him? You were in a class above him, then. Oh, thank you, John, those are sweet words, yes, we all took it quite hard, Carly most of all, I think."

"Mom!" I was standing at the kitchen door, completely flustered. I felt myself shaking, and I didn't know if it was the intimacy of their conversation or the fact that my mother could make much better small talk than me, that John looked so fantastic, that Jamie's tutor was about to appear and I didn't know how to handle that, or that I hadn't gotten any exercise in two days and I felt like I was going to burst. Mainly, it was the fact that I would never talk about my brother with some evil lawyer attempting to get a horrid woman out of a contract on some ridiculous technicality and I was completely counting on the money from settlement to pay taxes and to live on because I'd spent everything else trying to look good in new clothes and on Christmas presents. Not to mention the zillion dollars spent on shrink appointments because Paul never paid the Knot like he promised, and I didn't pre-register with the insurance company, which I absolutely despised because they rejected all my claims as "after the fact."

"What are you doing?" I demanded of Mom, all flushed.

"Well, dear, calm right down. I was only offering the gentleman a cup of tea." She turned to him. "Although in my house, it would be time for a whiskey sour."

"Tea's fine. Thank you so much." He was watching me.

Mom started the kettle, and it was a comfort to have her there, actually, while Jamie sat in the kitchen window, waiting for his tutor.

"He's waiting for his tutor," I explained.

"Are you a date?" Jamie asked.

"No," I replied, sharply.

"Why not, Mom?"

"Jamie..." Mother's voice warned.

"I want you to go out with someone nice. Are you nice?" Jamie asked John.

"Very nice," John replied. "I don't think your mother's convinced, though."

"Do you like kids?" asked Jamie.

"That's enough, Jamie," my mother told him.

John looked a little confused, unsure of what to do. I didn't think he wanted to pull out his legal papers right then, so I decided to take advantage of the situation. I'd make him like all of us, or at least feel sorry for us. How can you sue someone when you've been in his or her kitchen for tea?

"Here she comes!" Jamie announced, as if a guest were arriving for a surprise party.

I turned to John and spoke like Jackie Kennedy, "I am so sorry I couldn't speak to you earlier. My life is quite chaotic, you see. But thank you for taking the time to meet me at my home. Now, how may I help you?" I wasn't going to give him even the slightest indication that I would have fucked him on the floor of Austin Grill if he had asked me. I acted like a completely different person. After all, he was the lawyer who was about to practically ruin my life for some nasty bitch.

Kerry burst through the kitchen door. "Oh, crap, it's only you," Jamie greeted her.

"Jamie," Mom admonished, again.

"I hate you too." Kerry kind of shoved him. "Mom, my leotard ripped. I told you I needed a new one, didn't I? Everyone laughed at me. And all my Girl Scout emblems came off." She faced me, hot red, about to cry, waiting for a motherly hug, waiting for a "so sorry, honey bear, I'll make it all okay, I promise." So that's what I did. I scooped her up as she showed me her Girl Scout shirt, and it was quite embarrassing, since all of her little emblems for "Best Attitude" or "Graduated from Brownies with honors" were hanging precariously by a thread or gone completely.

"Kerry, darling," Mom exclaimed, clearly horrified. "Who did this dreadful sewing job?" She looked at me. *Oops*, she seemed to say. *Sorry*, she mouthed.

"Mommy did." She pointed her finger at me and, knowing she had a sympathetic audience, dissolved in tears.

"Your fault," Jamie told her. "Everyone knows Mommy can't sew."

"Or cook," accused Kerry, taking advantage of the situation to get out all of her anger at her mother, who had obviously chased her beloved father right out of the house and sent away the lovely French lady who made homemade cookies every Friday and knew how to sew.

"Kerry," I said in a soft voice that clearly meant, *if you don't stop embarrassing me you won't eat for a week.* "We'll fix this later. Promise."

The kitchen doorbell rang and Miss Donovan, whom I had never met, which was a whole other embarrassing story since every mother really should meet her child's tutor, was standing at the door. But I'd forgotten the appointment, and it was only after she received a check from Paul—who explained that I was "just like that" as if to issue a warning that I was actually insane—which she had cashed to make sure it was good, that she decided to take Jamie on as her pupil. A sympathetic gesture, no doubt.

I couldn't stand her from the minute I saw her—a fifty-ish prude of a woman with stockings so thick she could have been a nurse. She looked angry from the start, huffing as if she'd been forced to jog to our house. "Your driveway is so slippery, I had to walk up," were her first words.

"Everyone else seemed to make it." That wasn't nice, so I added, "Tea, perhaps?" and smiled. She declined, so Jamie and I led her upstairs to his fake room. "I'll be right back," I assured Mr. John Davenport. Hey, it was on Slovinski's bill, what did I care? And besides, I didn't want to make anything easy for him.

He'd insisted on this meeting in the first place. I, of course, would rather have avoided the entire affair.

Upon examining our guest room, Miss Nosy said that she was quite surprised at the "scarcity of distractions," and with that, Jamie started giggling and turned all flushed. She looked at him a bit suspiciously, but she had to believe us. What else could she do?

Everything would have been fine if she hadn't asked to use the bathroom and the trap door to the attic hadn't fallen down when she slammed the bathroom door. When she opened the door back up to see what the noise was, three of the five garbage bags fell on her head, and Jamie's things were strewn all over the hall.

"You didn't tie the bags? Jesus, Jamie!" He never finished a task! "We're so sorry. Are you okay?"

She didn't look okay. She looked livid. She'd lost her balance when the bags hit her and ended up on the floor with Jamie's old clothes, posters, stereo, and shoes all around her. Now she was huffing away, trying to get up with dignity, knowing we could see right up her blue skirt. Jamie and I were too stunned to help her right at the instant we realized she was on the ground. Everything had happened really quickly. I wasn't too upset about it until I remembered she could sue me, and one lawsuit was more than enough.

"Are you okay, really?" Serves you right for being so nosy! I wanted to add.

"I am fine." She glared at us, finally managing to stand. Without a word, she marched into Jamie's fake room, grabbed her briefcase and pocketbook, and marched down the stairs, past Mother, Kerry, and Mr. Davenport and right out the door.

Mom took Kerry upstairs to sew on her emblems and organize her clothes and give her a bath. Jamie was returning his room to its natural condition, and I sat down opposite John Davenport, who hadn't uttered a word during the whole affair.

"More tea?" I inquired. He indicated that he was fine, thank you.

"She doesn't have a case," I stated.

"You weren't lying when you said you were busy."

"No. I don't lie. I try not to, anyway."

"My client wants out of this, Ms. Macalister," he said and looked down. It seemed surreal—so totally different than the night we met, when everything felt so magical, like we were floating—and now he couldn't even look me in the eye. I hadn't felt that attracted to someone except Alex in my entire life. Now it was "Ms. Macalister."

Suddenly I was too tired to cope. I didn't know the contract well enough, obviously. My daughter was hurt and my son was humiliated and my mother was shocked at the dishes, and Paul wasn't paying alimony and I needed to fix dinner and I couldn't let my mother think I was falling apart because if she worried any more about me she'd definitely have a stroke since I was her only child and I had to be happy and strong for her no matter what.

And John was just another asshole lawyer who couldn't give a damn about me or what was right or anything else as long as he made his money.

"Let her out then. You won. Tell her congratulations." I got up, trying to show him to the door. "Just fax my manager about what base I didn't cover. They'll give me a penalty, the owners will survive, precious Slovinski can go to hell, and you'll make your fee. Okay? Be a hero. That's fine with me."

I stood by the kitchen door, waiting for him to leave.

"Mom? I'm starving!" Jamie called from upstairs.

"Hush, child, she's in a meeting," we heard my mom admonish him.

John Davenport finally looked up at me with those brown eyes boring into mine, and his held such compassion I was tempted to just let it all out and scream, "No, I'm not in control of this and you'd better leave right now before I ask you to carry me out of here to some hotel where I can collapse and have those broad shoulders surround me and that voice of yours assure me that everything will be fine and then you'd take Jamie to his tutor and sort through the bills and hold out a shield against the collection agencies and make sure the puppy's had shots and the roof isn't collapsing!"

Still he didn't move.

"Go! I cave. No need to prolong it." I was getting angry.

He stood up. "It would come down to your word against hers, and you have documentation to prove your case. No client of mine's going to lie under oath."

We stared at each other. Neither of us moved.

"I'll let her know."

"Mommy!" Jamie called down again. John shook my hand, holding it for a moment longer than one would expect, and then he walked out the door, closing it gently behind him.

"YES!" I shrieked after I heard John's car leave. I raced upstairs and told everyone and hugged Mom as hard as I could. The kids were all excited because I was. I called Ellie first and she was ecstatic.

"Carly, I am so proud of you, girl. You did it!" I giggled. "You're going to win Rookie of the Year, I know it. This is going to put you over the top." Forget the award, I want the money, I thought. But I felt so happy that she was proud of me.

Mom had hidden champagne in the fridge "just in case" and we popped it open. Alex came by after I called him and so did Tina and we had a little celebration. "I can do this," I thought, relieved and giddy. "I can make it without a husband after all." Then I remembered we'd be living in a gutter if it weren't for my mother, Tina, and Alex.

ELEVEN

Time to look for a new nanny and get back to work in order to:

A. Become sane again

B. Stop relying on my mother and my friends

Problem: lack of nanny so lack of work to make money to pay nanny

The dreaded April fifteenth deadline was two weeks away and everything would have been perfectly fine if I had saved enough money to pay the IRS. Unfortunately, I was going to pay my taxes with the money I earned from the Maria Slovinski settlement, but the check had to go to the office first to be processed and the receptionist was in charge of this procedure and she had thrown my flowers in the trash. It wasn't looking good.

The Knot called that evening. "I was going over my notes and I was wondering if you were taking your new medication."

"The only thing I need right now is cash," I told him.

He was silent.

"I haven't tried it yet," I admitted. I didn't even know where I had put the prescription.

He suggested I find it, bring it to the pharmacy, have it filled, and then take it. I told him four tasks seemed a lot for one lousy prescription.

The next day, under Dr. Knot's orders, I attended an adult ADD meeting. Everyone was late. People kept interrupting one another. Or they lost their train of thought. I felt sorry for them all. Then they had the nerve to say that I had the worst symptoms. Just because this one lady kept clicking her pen and another was chewing gum, and finally, I couldn't stand it anymore and I started shrieking at them, "God, you are so annoying!" They all stopped and looked at me. I thought it was okay to do that. Apparently not. It felt good, though.

Basically, I believe the Knot was overreacting regarding my propensity to become angry and lose control. I was picking up the phone to tell him that his diagnosis was way out of line when the phone rang and it was Paul. He asked me out for dinner.

Dutch, of course.

"You take every floozy in this city to dinner and you won't take your wife? And why the hell would I go to dinner with you anyway?"

"Because we have to discuss business." He paused and made a huge concession. "Fine, Carly, I'll treat. Now let's be civil about this. Oriental at seven on Thursday?"

Our favorite place. God, I wished I could say I had plans on Thursday. And Thursday seemed really far away and I needed to know what he wanted.

"Busy Thursday. Tonight I'm free. Bring your credit card." And I hung up. He hated when I did that. But I didn't want him to say, "No, I'm busy tonight" and then I'd get no sleep until Thursday because he was up to something.

Dressed to the nines. Large, deep eyes. Make-up impeccable. Hair in place and shiny.

"Are you going to the White House or something?" asked the hairdresser.

I felt like I was going to the guillotine.

Paul was late. I sat at the bar and ordered a Coke, but kept going back and forth to the bathroom to check on my appearance. The bartender was getting suspicious, like I was doing drugs or something, because I was acting furtive and shifty.

Paul finally swept in, shaking the bartender's hand like they were old friends. Of course, Paul lived in D.C. now, free as a bird. He probably knew every bartender and waitress in the whole damn city.

We shook hands. He looked so handsome in his navy blue jacket and the tie I gave him for Father's Day when he was a father.

"Well, Carly, I must say, you look ...really...quite nice." There was a look between us. He was still attracted to me, definitely.

We were led to a table overlooking the city. It looked like it was winking at me.

We sat across from each other. Paul ordered two martinis, just like we used to. I missed someone ordering for me. I would have to remember to drink mine very slowly. This dinner had to go well. I had to act like a lady at all times, so his impression of me would be branded in his mind of a mature, brilliant, attractive, alluring woman. I'd also be light and funny. He used to love that about me. And he'd remember why he married me.

"My, has Carly changed. Or was she always this clever and beautiful?" he would think, furious at himself for letting me go. He'd be tortured over this—trying everything to get me back, to have his family back.

We were seated at the best table—a corner table with windows on all sides of the city. No one else was near us. Paul and I skirted subjects, like playing in a minefield. The drinks came.

We toasted and laughed a bit about old times and different cute stories about Jamie and Kerry. He even made some self-depreciating joke about going to sex-addicts anonymous.

I put the martini glass precariously up to my lips, all relaxed, giving him a seductive look, thankful I had gone for a manicure when Paul leaned forward. "Carly, I need to ask you for an annulment."

Splat! The entire swallow landed right on his nose.

"A WHAT?"

He wiped it off, unfazed. "You see, Dawn is Catholic and—"

"She's also twenty-two. You've known her a month."

"And I may want to become engaged…"

"You have two kids, Paul. Remember?" My voice rose just a little.

He looked around and then gave me a look. "Be reasonable, please. You know how I feel about your temper."

"Fuck you," I said quietly, like steel. "You can't take a marriage of fifteen years and two children and pretend it never existed so that you can get your dick sucked any time you'd like."

"Carly, Jesus," he hissed.

The waitress approached us. He called her by her name, of course. In a few minutes, Susie. A little wink. I wanted to reach over the table and strangle him. "Carly. We both know our marriage is over. Now there's a chance I might want to start a new family and Dawn, for religious reasons, insists on—"

Paul and I split up and he goes and fucks every girl in the city (like he had the whole time we were married, I remembered) and now he's in love with some Dawn chick who would be my children's step-monster and I haven't even gotten kissed yet. Fuck. And now he wants me to pretend our family didn't even exist?

"You told me this in a public place so I wouldn't physically harm you."

"Exactly. Now calm down. We've talked to the priests and it's done all the time."

"Right. Sure. Like who?" I demanded. "No marriage can get annulled if the couple has children, for Christ sakes."

"Don't swear when we're talking about this. And in fact, I do know of someone."

"Who?" I was curious.

"Ted Kennedy," he answered triumphantly.

"Wow. To Joan?"

"Three children and everything." He was smiling.

I was quiet, for once. The waitress came back. He ordered two shrimp cocktails like we always had and two strip steaks.

I tried to think clearly. I needed to be reasonable. I leaned forward. "Start a new family? Look at your kids, Paul. You see them, finally, on Wednesdays and every other weekend. But you tell them you'll be at their games or recitals and you never make it. You hire sitters when they come to visit. What the hell are you thinking? Are you going to annul *them?*"

He had the nerve to shrug it off. "Well, it's how Dawn wants it, so there's not much I can do."

The place settings arrived with the shrimp. Paul was at his most charming, "Thank you, thank you, Susie, isn't it? Thought so. Everything is fine, thank you." Big smile. "Oh, I know you haven't seen us in a long time…Yes, we did used to come here together…quite often, yes…Oh? Yes, you are right; you were our waitress when we came for out fifteenth anniversary. Yes, that was great."

I looked out the window to the city. Such a beautiful city. Paul's real self must have gotten buried so far down that he had lost touch with reality.

"Does she know you fuck everything in a skirt?"

His lips tightened. He looked very, very angry. "We have an understanding."

"How fortunate." I tried to think straight. "Look," I told him calmly, "None of this mess is my problem. But it is my problem because you've apparently decided not to take responsibility for your very own children, who unfortunately are innocent victims of all this and need their father and I will not let you hurt them anymore than you already have."

Talking to air.

"I'm afraid I have to insist on the annulment. I've started the paperwork with the church."

I'd love an annulment, asshole. "I can't do that to the kids."

He stared at me. I stared at him.

"Yes. I'm afraid I must insist, for Dawn's sake."

For Dawn's sake, you will legally never have been married…

"I said no."

"I said yes."

"Fuck you."

"No thanks."

Okay. That was it. I picked up the steak knife and fiddled with it. I had that look in my eyes, like when I socked him in the nose.

"I think you would look better without a nose at all," I mumbled, loud enough for him to hear me. I pretended like I was going into an altered state.

Paul was watching me closely. Paul had always been a scared sissy down deep. He never played football. He played the piano. When we got robbed he made me go down to the kitchen with the gun.

"You know I can be very, very irrational. And as you know, I have a nasty, nasty temper. I'm dangerous, Paul." I flicked the knife in my hand so the light would reflect on it. "Your behavior has caused serious mental problems for me. I must admit, I have homicidal thoughts. Dr. Knot is very concerned." Then I jerked to my feet and lunged like I was going to stab him. He screamed and fell backwards in his chair onto the carpet, and I put the knife down so quickly no one saw it and Paul looked like a complete fool who must have been so drunk he fell over in his chair. "You're going to be there for those kids, Paul. You're going to take care of them."

I went over and poured the entire martini right in his face as he was trying to stand, and then I marched out of the restaurant.

The next morning I received a package from Paul's lawyer outlining Paul's proposed settlement for our divorce case.

I didn't even know for sure until last night that we were definitely going through with it.

I almost refused to accept it, but I had answered "yes" when the man asked me if I was Catherine Russell Macalister, so he made me sign his little sheet of paper and take the package like I was being subpoenaed.

I sat at the kitchen table and opened it up.

The language was typical lawyer—incomprehensible, but I got the gist. He wanted an annulment due to the fact that I had not performed my wifely obligations properly; he wanted the home since maintaining two residences was beyond his means financially; no alimony since I was currently employed and had displayed the ability to make my own money; and the lowest child support allowed under D.C. law—enough to support the kids if they went to school naked and ate one meal a day.

Detachment and disbelief are two of God's best gifts to human beings. Sometimes when something terrible happens, you just can't believe it. It doesn't sink in.

I calmly called the most influential and powerful woman in Washington that I knew: my mother. Perhaps Paul was stupid enough not to realize it. But when push comes to shove…

The following afternoon I was seated opposite one of the top woman divorce lawyers in the country. I also have steely business sense when needed, I realized, because real estate isn't just about showing pretty houses. Slovinksi was the only client that almost slipped through my fingers. But she didn't.

I sat across from Ms. Lydia Parker at exactly four o'clock that afternoon—a woman who commanded respect with her smooth, professional style and calm voice. She had shoulder-length black hair, glasses, and was most likely around fifty-five. She was quite pretty and impeccably dressed. Her corner office overlooked the Potomac River and the Kennedy Center, and the ticket for my parking was stamped upon arrival by one of her four assistants. It was a Wednesday, so Paul had the kids. How helpful of him.

Ms. Parker was skimming the contract. "He wants to uproot his own children from their home and school?" she asked, talking to herself. "He asks for an annulment after fifteen years of marriage. That's very interesting." She stood up. "Let me handle this. I can't guarantee anything. But this is one of the most abusive proposals I've ever seen. My instruction to you is, don't say a word to him and don't do a thing. I'll call you after I've looked into this."

I thought I'd be stuck in there for hours and the meeting lasted eight minutes. She was hired.

"Too bad Timmy can't surprise me on seventieth birthday. You know, sometimes spirits come back and visit."

Silence. I'd stopped by to thank Mom for her help with the lawyer.

"Too bad," I finally said.

"He'll be there, one way or another." We both were still. "Timmy won't be there in person, of course," Mom continued, "because he's a spirit, but he'll give me a sign. I'm quite sure." She resumed chopping cucumbers.

"I wish I felt that way. He never comes to visit me." *Carly, you are the most self-centered woman ever born. She lost her child; can you imagine losing one of yours?*

I shuddered.

"Well, you're still young and he's there, you just don't see it yet. Your father is the exact same way. What do you think, that when a body dies so does the soul? That would be ridiculous."

I walked over to the table and picked up a picture of Timmy and me skiing in Utah. I was fifteen and he was eighteen. Timmy was turned slightly toward the camera and wore an expression of careless joy with his signature trace of sadness draped over his slanted green eyes. He was by far the most gorgeous boy ever created. We were at the top of Snowbird after taking the very first tram up, even though Timmy hadn't gone to bed until five. Mom had trained us well: No matter what time you do or do not get to bed the night before, be the first ones on the lift.

"Do you feel him around, really?" I asked.

"Absolutely." Her voice sounded strained. "It's so fucking unfair, that's all."

"It sure as hell is."

Dad was in the den attempting to assemble a large robot that supposedly could carry your golf clubs with a remote control. Apparently, this gigantic automatic caddy would follow him around the golf course and hand him clubs. He looked pretty overwhelmed trying to put it together, with pieces spread all over the den and his headphones on. We sat in the living room with the food and drinks and tried to coax him to join us, but he just frowned and pointed to the instruction book.

For her seventieth birthday, Mom told me, all she wanted (besides a new sports car) was for me to "find a wonderful life." By that, of course, she meant a man. No pressure. Just find one. "Before my seventieth birthday, that's all I really want." That might be difficult since I'd decided I could never have a man see my home (too messy) or meet my children (they'd deliberately humiliate me). When they move out (probably at ages forty and forty-one, which means I'll be sixty-eight) I'll move into a brand new apartment. I'm sure I'll meet someone great. I'll be almost as old as my mother.

That night, I woke up from this dream where I was talking to Alex. We were swimming at the time. This is what I love about dreams...you can swim, talk, and ride horses in the ocean all at the same time.

Anyway, in the dream Alex was telling me I was a hopeless romantic who only wanted chocolates and flowers. He said I avoided real life. Then he pointed to the dream as an example. "See? Even your dreams are romantic. Swimming, riding horses..." I found this unfair, since I had included him in the dream and then he'd used it against me. You have to be so careful with men.

"Can I tell you what I hate?" I asked the Knot. "I hate to mail packages. I hate to sleep."

"Many people hate to sleep."

"It means the end of something, kind of like a surrender. You look forward to it, and then you have to confront it."

The Knot had temporarily given up on dealing with my past. I told him I had won the case against Slovinski and received a sterling silver picture frame from my manager at a sales meeting because I'd "exemplified the importance of writing a fool-proof contract and handled the situation professionally and with integrity."

"You won an award?"

"I guess, but the big thing was that I won 'Rookie of the Year,' so I guess I'll get something then, since it's a huge luncheon in September and it goes in the Post."

He smiled and studied me. He did seem impressed, which made me happy. "It seems you're successful without even trying. How do you feel about that?"

"What a shrinky question. I feel like it happened to someone else."

"You own all your faults and shrug off all your talents."

"Puritan ethic, I guess."

"You're allowed to shine. You're allowed to be happy."

"That happens sometimes."

It seemed paradoxical to me. One was supposed to be humble. After all, any gifts were given to us. That's what we're taught. Yet we're supposed to have confidence and love ourselves and forgive ourselves. We're supposed to visualize success but live in the present.

The Knot asked me to write a list:

Five Reasons to Be Single

1. Don't have to cook for him all the time

2. Don't have to sleep with him

3. More room in house

4. Have hope you'll meet someone you like one day

5. Can do what you want, like be messy

Five Reasons to Be Married

1. Security. More money if two people than one

2. Someone who'll drive you home from a party

3. Someone to go to a party with

4. Someone who can take you to drop your car off for repair

5. Convenient babysitter

I handed him the piece of paper. "That's it?" he asked.

"I think so. Is this supposed to make me feel better?"

"That's not the entire purpose. Aware, maybe."

"I like unaware. Unaware's fine."

"You knew you were in pain."

"But I didn't want to dwell on it!" I paused. "My mother believes in angels."

"That might be a great comfort to her. "

"She thinks Timmy comes around in different forms."

"What do you think?"

"I think time's up." I stood up. Why did I bring up Timmy?

He stayed seated. "You're avoiding the rest of the story."

I sat back down. "There was a huge fight. Timmy drowned afterwards." I paused. "Would you like to have sex?"

"That is a completely natural reaction," he assured me.

"I was only kidding," I told him.

He smiled. We were quiet.

"It's just nothing in the world could be sadder."

"You have to let go of the past."

I stood up. "Fuck you." I turned and left.

TWELVE

John Davenport called just as I walked in the door. At first I was terrified he'd found a way to sue me even though the case was over. Instead, he asked, "Do you like boats?"

"Broad question, don't you think?" thinking, "does he mean a rowboat in a swamp or a private yacht in the Caribbean?"

"Hmm. True. But if I tell you more than that you'll say no."

"Okay, I believe you. No."

"I'll give you a hint. They're skinny and dangerous; they can be a little tipsy on occasion, but that's what makes them exciting and sexy." He paused. "Just like you."

I laughed. "You rehearsed this. Typical lawyer."

"It's your weekend off, right?" From the kids, he meant. Interesting. He was right. I was stuck on "dangerous."

"Not those things that turn you upside down and you can't get out because you're strapped in?" I hesitated. "Please don't say kayak."

"Kayak."

"Forget it."

I had been in a kayak once in my life. It flipped over and I either had to be like Houdini to extract myself upside down and drowning from of all ropes and knots. The other choice was to be a chicken and raise your right hand and pray that the person you were with liked you enough to come over and "right the boat."

"I'm not taking you to a movie, so you don't have a choice."

Pretty smart. I hated going to the movies. You had to wait in a line. People kicked the back of your seat and smacked popcorn in your ear. You had to stay still for a really long time. That's why I only went to really terrible movies; they were less crowded.

"No, no, kayaking sounds…if you're trying to kill me just say so."

"No, I just want you wet and close to naked."

Late Friday afternoon, John and I were in two kayaks on the Potomac River. It was awesome. I was sheet-white stuffed into a black wetsuit with a gigantic red helmet, wearing practically no make-up since I didn't want it running all over the place when I got soaked or crashed into a bunch of rocks, tied into this ridiculous orange contraption with ropes and paddles flying everywhere, wobbly going around in circles because I couldn't get the paddle rhythm down at all, noticing John glide through the water like he was born on a kayak, and confronting rapids that looked like tidal waves.

John was watching and called out, "So, do you want to hear about my dark side?"

I thought that was very funny. "Is this your way of weeding out first dates?" I called back.

But the fact that I looked absurd and couldn't even maneuver the thing in perfectly still water was nothing compared to the Timmy-died-drowning head-trip, which was making me slightly ill.

"Confront your demons, baby. You can do anything," Timmy used to say when he was all pumped up.

At the end of our first shoot—which I did magnificently, I might add—John said, "See? I knew you'd make it." Well, I should hope so, since the alternative was death.

John opened a bottle of wine in the car after we'd made three trips down the rapids where we carried the kayaks on our shoulders back up the river after each run. I had one of those dead-to-the-bone feelings one would have after five hours in the ocean riding menacing waves or a day of skiing in a snowstorm so thick that almost everyone else had gone inside and you're the last group to enter the lodge for après ski and your legs shake under the table. It's the best feeling in the world.

Hmm. I looked over at him. I felt all tingly, like I had to have him right then and there. He looked at me the same way and we reached for each other and both broke out laughing—the two of us attempting to kiss like seals since we still had our wetsuits on.

John started driving to his house, where we were going to change and go to dinner. At one stoplight, though, he pulled me to him and gave me the ideal French kiss, flicking his tongue around mine until I moaned a little. What a perfect place to give someone a test kiss. It doesn't get awkward because the light changes.

I loved John's house—it didn't need any work. It had an open floor design, a great stereo system, a trendy kitchen, and a full basement full of play toys like a pool table, a dartboard, and huge leather couches, a widescreen TV, and a full bar with barstools. The second floor had two large bedrooms with skylights and walk-in closets, two full state-of-the art bathrooms with gigantic Jacuzzi tubs, surround sound music, a steam shower, and skylights as well, and yet it didn't seem tacky or too modern at all. What a fantastic bachelor pad. Or bachelorette pad, I thought, feeling jealous. This was definitely my dream home. I kept this all to myself, of course.

"I'm buying it if you ever sell," I told him, wandering around the place like it was a palace.

"Make sure you have a good agent."

"The best," I replied.

He put me in the guest room to take a shower and change. Oh no. Everything had a place. He was the type who put a picture frame back at the exact same angle, and the cabinets were so organized that he'd know if you snuck into one for an Oreo.

"I hired a maid service for three days, so don't think it always looks like this." John's voice echoed from outside the door. Did he read minds?

John had told me to bring a change of clothes for dinner, which presented its own set of problems since I didn't know where we were going, but I thought the hell with it and brought jeans that fit me just the way I wanted and a cashmere sweater and topaz and silver earrings and my platform shoes to make him have to notice how long my legs were. And make-up. I got out of the shower and there, laid out on the bed, were red silk pajamas with a note. "Reservations are for 8, so if you want to relax and have a cocktail first, put these perfectly respectable pj's on and meet me at the bar." Wow.

John had fresh shrimp and brie with hot bread plus the blender going with you-know-what when I made my way in wonder down to the bar in his basement that wasn't like any basement I'd ever been in. I was home, baby. (When did I start calling myself baby? I wondered.) I felt like a sex goddess in those silky, slinky things I was wearing with my hair all dry and wild and just the right touch of eyeliner and lipstick—just a touch… Oh God, Alex was right! I should have gotten some practice with this dating business. This was my very first date since I was eighteen years old and met Paul on my first day of college.

John was in silk pajamas as well. His were dark grey. He looked up and smiled, handing me a golden margarita with fresh lime. "It's the only drink I was pretty sure you liked."

"Hah. Very intuitive." Still, I was so impressed it was ridiculous. He came up close, silk-to-silk. "Cheers to you, Carly Macalister—graceful, gorgeous, funny, sexy…" He had this sense of humor that got me, "…brilliant, perceptive, gutsy," he cooed between kisses.

"You just want to get laid."

He shook his head. "Wrong. I'm a perfect gentleman. We'll leave for dinner right now."

"Forget it. I need to beat you at pool."

It took at least an hour before John had me on his wide, delicious leather couch that felt like heaven next to silk pajamas and a hard, lean body that was driving me crazy. All those delicious sensations woke up a Carly that never had a chance to come out and say, "Boo." It felt so good, John felt so good. His hands and tongue were everywhere. I was moaning, "Oh my God, you feel so good! Oh my God." I couldn't help it. Didn't care. Never wanted anyone more. We missed our reservation. Technically, he stayed a gentleman like he promised. It's all a matter of semantics.

John and I didn't do much that weekend. I may have left his bed three or four times for a little frolicking and party-time in his basement—dancing a little, shooting pool, playing darts, making bets, concocting cocktails, fucking on the couch, the floor, on top of the bar, in the bathtub, in the shower, eating lamb chops one night, or maybe that was in the morning, feeding each other cheesecake, taking all phones off the hook, drawing all shades, half sleeping with John and he was on me again and I was clawing his back or he was slipping down on me or I was under the covers—or we were both upside down and inside out, it's hard to be too specific about the timeline.

Sunday afternoon we ventured out to Georgetown for brunch before I had to go home. I could barely move. He led me to a corner table where it was dark and cozy. I'd gotten used to the dark and cozy by then.

"I'm leaving a glass slipper."

"No need. I know how to find you."

THIRTEEN

John and I were together every chance we could be after that first weekend, which for me meant Wednesday nights and every other weekend. Not that I didn't adore my children, but I suddenly felt like a caged animal, for God's sake! Paul could run around all the time fucking and partying and there I was, horny all the time, counting the hours for every other weekend? How fair was that?

When we had our time together, John and I did normal, relaxing things. We left his house at least once a weekend to eat. He was a fantastic lover, so why would I want to do anything else? "Make up for lost time" was my motto. I'd played tennis, gone biking, and swam enough for a lifetime. I only wanted one thing.

When I arrived at John's home early Friday evenings, it was like entering another planet—no kids, no bills, no cooking, no homework, no office, no annoying phone calls or problems— just body-to-body erotic, spine-chilling pleasure, scrumptious food fed to me in bed, laughter, great music, an endless game of pool or darts in his basement, a ceremony of some new concoction of a drink involving alcohol, and no concept of time at all.

"Maybe this is what happens after you die," I thought hope-fully, but which would it be? Heaven or hell? Is this acting bad or good? I, personally, not being religious in a traditional sense, but with a special connection with Jesus (as long as I was alone with him and not with a bunch of other people taking all his attention), had a long talk with him, and Jesus thought I was doing exactly what I was supposed to be doing.

The only downside and upside about my relationship with John Davenport was that it was strictly based on fantasy. As I drove home at the end of a weekend, I always felt terrible. It was like two separate lives that I couldn't merge.

This realization would have put my mother into cardiac arrest. I tried to downplay the fact that I was even dating John, but she was so nosy that she knew exactly how much time I spent with him—but thank God she had no clue how we spent our time. I had to lie about that one, being creative and smart so she wouldn't catch me lying. She didn't give me a choice, though. She shouldn't have asked many questions in the first place. She was my *mother*, not Tina.

Mom's new goal in life, knowing I was spending so much time with John Davenport, was for us to get engaged NOW, terrified he'd suddenly get to know the real me and move to Korea. She didn't *say* this, of course, but I could read the woman like a book. I felt like breaking up with him just to annoy her, but that would be, as she said, "shooting myself in the foot."

In any case, I decided not to invite John to Mother's seventieth birthday. Who knows how my mother would act?

On June 15th, Mom finally turned seventy—a day she claimed she'd been dreading her entire life. "You felt the same way at sixty, sixty-five, and so on," I said to deaf ears.

Dad decided to throw her an elaborate affair, catered and everything, which everyone thought was very cute because it meant he actually remembered it was her birthday and was going to make an effort of some sort. Dad has never even made his own cocktail. He pretends he doesn't know how. Once I saw him slip into the kitchen and whip up a perfect whiskey sour in about a second.

At Mom's party, you'd think we were attending a funeral. Mom dressed in a black suit and refused to accept presents or cards. We brought them for her anyway, in case her curiosity got the better of her, but she didn't touch them. She put on this ridiculous frozen smile for the friends we'd invited and reminded me that most of her good friends were dead. I whispered to her that if she kept making comments like that in front of her guests, she wouldn't have any friends left at all.

Dad, on the other hand, was jovial for most of the evening, telling the same jokes he'd told at every family gathering since we were kids. He opened all of Mom's presents and even put on some Cole Porter and danced around the living room a few times. This actually made her laugh, so he swooped her up and swung her around the room crooning "Happy birthday to you..."

When Alex arrived, I felt like running upstairs and hiding like a guilty child. He looked gorgeous, first of all, entering the hallway with flowers and three huge presents. I hadn't seen him since, well, since John. I avoided his calls or acted really busy. Alex knew.

Mom rushed up to kiss and hug him, all flushed and happy he had made it since he was supposedly scheduled for the ER that night, according to Mom. She might have made the other guests wonder what was wrong with *them,* since her reaction to their arrival was a stone-faced greeting. After Alex became untangled from his presents and flowers and his coat and my mother, his eyes met mine. They held a sadness and defeat. My lower lip started to quiver. I loved him so much. John was physical. I loved Alex so, so much. But it was too late. That's what his look told me, anyway. I'd betrayed him.

This was my mother's night, though, so we faked our way through it. The party got much better as Mom finally let it all go and became her festive, light, gay social self again. There were lots of toasts, delicious food and wine, Dad danced around a bit with the ladies, and Mom finally opened her presents that Dad hadn't gotten to. She handled it beautifully, not interrupting the party but reacting to her gifts just enough so people knew she appreciated them. Mom was back in her element momentarily, enjoying herself, playing hostess, until it was time for the cake. That's when, after the candles and everything, my father stood up and made a toast.

Dad announced, after everyone quieted down to give him his or her full attention, that after fifty years of marriage, he had decided to go to marriage counseling, with or without his wife. But, happy birthday.

There was an awkward silence.

"Why?" I finally asked, since he was waiting for this.

"She hates her truck," Dad explained.

Mom threw her arms up in the air, spilling half her wine all over poor Alex, "Oh, Lord, just because you buy me a huge white truck, making me look like the goddamn ice-cream man, doesn't mean I hate *you*."

"You screamed at me for over two hours! You said you wanted a divorce!"

"I said I wanted a sports car or a trip helicopter skiing. You know I don't want a divorce." Dad wasn't convinced. "I'll just trade that contraption in for something more fitting. I'm not trading *you* in." She smiled and went over and gave him a hug. "Happy birthday to me…" she sang softly in his ear.

Dad was still pouting. "It's a safe truck," he mumbled. He looked so cute. He had a way of pouting that made him look like Snoopy. "You drive too fast. I thought it was a wonderful present."

Mom thought about this. She'd hurt his feelings. "I know what we'll do. I'll give the truck to *you,* instead."

Dad's obsessed with any new vehicle so he seemed happy about the compromise, and the birthday crisis was over.

Everyone acted like this was all completely normal and started talking and laughing and being gay again. The music was back on. I looked around and Alex was gone. He hadn't even said goodbye.

I wanted to run after him, chase him down the street, pound on his door, and scream in his window. Clearly, I had gone insane. John was just an escape from reality. John was my sexual wake-up call. John and I both knew it on some level. He would want his own kids, not mine. We were from two different universes. Why hadn't I realized it before? I had, but why hadn't I *really* realized it instead of acting like a giggly, horny, oblivious bubblehead?

I thought I was going to scream, smiling and saying good-night to the guests. I had to get out of there.

"Night, Mom. Love you. Happy birthday." Hug to Dad. "Night, Dad. You did a great job. Love you guys. Gotta go. Late for the sitter."

John was the one who brought out my wild side. I wanted to be that way with Alex. John was my practice. Alex was the real thing.

Or, maybe I didn't have a clue what was going on. That could be the problem.

FOURTEEN

This had not been my year for animals. First, Jackie the Jack Russell swallowed some of Jamie's Ritalin and spent the night at the vet's for observation. This was a humiliating event, since first I was the laughing stock of the entire vet office for insisting on bringing in a Jack Russell puppy because she was acting hyperactive.

"All Jack Russell puppies are hyperactive," the receptionist explained like I was a moron.

"This is different," I insisted.

"But—" she tried to protest.

"I'm coming."

I got there and poor Jackie was running into walls and could not stop moving. The vet seemed quite disturbed and took me into a little room to ask me if I did cocaine or speed. No, no! My hands were getting sweaty because he didn't believe me. "This dog is on drugs." He paced back and forth waiting for me to confess when I remembered the Ritalin that Jamie spilled all over the kitchen floor that morning. I leapt up and hugged the vet. "It's Ritalin!"

They gave Jackie a shot to subdue her and kept her overnight for "tests and observation." I knew they just wanted to see if I was telling the truth.

Then Kerry's rabbit, Jake, dropped dead. The good news was the rabbit died peacefully of old age, which was a huge delight for me since this was the first time I'd ever been able to keep an animal long enough for him or her to die of old age. They usually died tragic deaths—such as jumping out of the sunroof of the car and landing in the water while we were taking a ferry across to Shelter Island (kitty #1), or strangling when Jamie took Jesse for a walk on his bunny leash (bunny #1), or collapsing from a drug overdose when Mother fed Jenny a Valium because she acted nervous on car trips (bunny #2). To actually have an animal die of natural causes, I felt, validated me as a perfectly capable and normal housewife.

Kerry, however, was inconsolable about Jake's passing, which seemed odd to me since I couldn't remember the last time she'd even noticed the poor animal, much less fed him or cleaned his cage. In fact, I was pretty sure Kerry had forgotten she *had* a rabbit, because ever since "My Space" she'd been living in front of her computer. She wouldn't even come out for meals unless I forced her to. Therefore, I was not particularly concerned when I told Kerry about Jake. It's just that the porch had collapsed into shambles on the same day, so she found the entire ordeal very traumatic.

What happened was, the very first day after Mom's birthday party, the children's second to last day at school, I'd planned to pack them up perfectly for their visit with their father at his family's estate in New Hampshire. Simultaneously, I planned to decide exactly what my feelings were for Alex and John. I had gotten up early and marched out to the newly renovated porch to enjoy a cup of coffee and feed Kerry's rabbit, Jake.

It was my sixth cup of coffee so I may have been over-thinking the situation when I went over to Jake's cage to feed him and he was dead. As I picked up his cage (I wasn't about to touch him) to move it inside while I figured out what to do with a dead rabbit, the entire porch started crackling and caving down on top of me while I scurried into the dining room before it flattened me completely. I looked back and the whole thing was in shambles.

Kerry had come home from school and noticed our former porch strewn in pieces all over the back lawn. She shrieked (thinking Jake had been crushed by the porch), "Oh my God, what about Jake?"

"Don't worry, dear," I told her somewhat proudly. "The porch didn't kill him. I found him dead this morning. He died of old age!"

I thought Kerry would be relieved, but she howled and cried and screamed for hours until I promised to have a rabbit funeral, but I told her we should wait until fall. "That's the problem with dying in the summer in Washington," I explained. "Everyone's away." I was really hoping she'd buy it, but, of course, she didn't. So I had to have the funeral.

The porch collapsed, to be honest, because I am very cheap when it comes to certain things, so the contractor (Phil) who built it may not have been particularly reliable. He was a patient of Alex's and his estimate was very low. The job was simple: replace the screens with glass. It took him three months. I hadn't been able to use my backyard all spring since it was strewn with nails, boards, ladders, siding, asbestos, and assorted tools.

Apparently Phil had difficulty with concentration, completing tasks, and visual perception. Alex finally admitted this. All I wanted was my simple screened porch back. Now, with the collapse of the entire porch, I had nothing. I called Alex, not feeling romantic like I had the night before in the least, and I told him he had to make this up to me by burying the rabbit and coming to the funeral, no excuses.

Three days later, the morning of the funeral party, I woke up anxious. The porch was still strewn in piles over the lawn, although Phil had promised he would have it all cleaned up. Still, Phil was sort of part of the family by then, so I invited him to the rabbit funeral.

I also hadn't planned the menu or bought any beverages, no maid was cleaning the place spotless, no sitter arriving for the kids, no gorgeous dry-cleaned outfit waiting in my closet, and Paul hadn't sent a cent in two weeks.

The first phone call arrived at 7:15 a.m. It was my mother (of course), which I let go into voice mail so I could hear it without wasting time talking. "Carly, my fabulous woman, Naomi, is coming over to help you clean and cook. Alex is getting the beverages; you make someone get the food. I want you to look drop-dead gorgeous tonight. Who knows who will be there?"

Next message: "Carly, this is your lawyer. Please call me regarding your progress obtaining a copy of your purchasing contract." Paul had taken both his copy and mine, the snake. This was a problem. I'd worry about the lawyer tomorrow.

Next message: "Carly, it is your mother. Call me before you look at the Post." I hadn't even gotten out of my pajamas yet.

I was making coffee, making lists of food and things to do, when I decided out of curiosity to slip down to the end of the driveway and pick up the Post to see what Mother was talking about.

I obliviously traipsed down my driveway in my pajamas to grab the paper when I noticed a gigantic man pounding a "FOR SALE" sign at the edge of the property and at least ten horribly aggressive women from the real estate firm that was our main competitor (can't name names for fear of a lawsuit, but I will say these girls were tacky and gave the real estate business a bad name) were creeping up my driveway like parasites.

"GO AWAY!" I screeched. "This house is NOT for sale!" I tore back to the house and grabbed Jamie's toy gun he'd gotten for Christmas and my phone. I ran back to the driveway. The guy, whose job was simply to plant "For Sale" posts, as well as the real estate agents, who looked terrified, saw me and were backing away. Since I was in the business, I knew them all, but at the time I didn't care on one level although at the same time I had the sense to call Ellie as I yelled, "Get that thing out of the ground right now!" to the gigantic man hammering in the sign. Then to the agents, in my pajamas and holding the gun, "Get off of my property before I lose my temper! Does everyone understand?"

Ellie answered the phone (after the terrified receptionist retrieved her from a meeting; the receptionist claims I threatened her, which I don't recall). "Carly!"

"Ellie!" I screeched. The post guy was extracting the sign. In the old days, I would most likely have been burnt to death as a witch. "Come here, Ellie, they're selling my house!"

I was hysterical. Ellie knew when I was in bad shape, and besides the fact that she was a true friend, she also knew I could be valuable to her, since for some God-forsaken reason I had beaten out six thousand agents and won "Rookie of the Year," which was great for our company but also was purely a reflection on Ellie's abilities to teach and motivate me, because if it weren't for Ellie I wouldn't have sold a thing. Regardless, she had her own reason to help me: her firm's reputation.

I turned and ran up the driveway before creating more damage, noting more and more cars with agents driving up to view the new listing in Chevy Chase, D.C., where homes sell in less than half a day. I ran into the house like I was a hounded celebrity. I called my mother: "Mother. Paul took all of my paperwork. Dad may be boring but he's meticulous. Ask him if he has the contract from our purchase of this house twenty years ago and get it to me now." Click.

Called lawyer. "Paul put the house on the market."

"Get me the paperwork if you can. No matter how that works, his action is illegal and I'll follow up."

"But the agents are here now!" Do not get hysterical with lawyer. "I'll find the contract," I told her in a calmer tone.

I looked outside and a limousine was in my driveway. A horrible showy agent? No one drives a limo. Food Paul ordered for un-agreed upon open house? Possible. Or the funeral consultant Paul ordered knowing I'd drop dead at all the pressure? Most likely. I peered out the window and involuntarily let out a scream.

Patrice appeared, impeccably dressed in a God-only-knows-which-designer outfit, large sunglasses, classy $300-plus hair-cut, Milano or whatever-they-are shoes, and twenty pounds thinner. Taking her time, as elegant as Audrey Hepburn, she stepped from the limo as the driver opened the door.

So I locked my door and ran upstairs two by two, leapt into the shower for thirty seconds, raced into the bedroom and threw on a dress, prayed someone who loved me had arrived (such as Ellie, Mom, or Alex), threw on a little make-up while ignoring the doorbell, and pranced down the steps imagining I was a queen. The Queen of Sheba. "Everyone outside my glorious home is a trivial snake to be squashed," I told myself. I opened the door.

"Patrice!" I screamed. I leapt into her arms and almost knocked her over before bursting into tears, dragging her into the house to block out all the nosy agents who had now encompassed the entire property like greedy paparazzi going after Britney Spears and collapsed on the kitchen floor, pulling her down with me. So much for dignity.

"I love you! I miss you so much!" I sobbed. Patrice looked baffled. "I mean I know I seem put together and everything, but underneath, I am a wreck!" I confessed. She was struggling to extract herself from me and stand up as I kept talking, "Where have you been? Don't you know how much I've worried about you? How could you even touch him? I thought you loved me!" I was definitely losing it.

Mom walked in. "Hi, Patrice," she said casually.

Then Ellie entered, shutting the door in a flash to block out prying agents. "Patrice! You look great. Carly, do you have your contract? Are you on it or not?"

Mother dramatically pulled a folder out of her purse. "Hello, Ellie, you look absolutely wonderful." Ellie and Mom hugged.

"Catherine! I cannot believe you! No one in this town looks more like a queen."

"What about me?" I screamed to everyone, in tears, on the floor, ignored, and in need of a little bit of sympathy and support.

Mom, Ellie, and Patrice stared down at me crouching on the floor like a Vietnam orphan. They didn't look disgusted or embarrassed for me. They actually looked concerned for the first time since Patrice and Paul had left so long ago.

Suddenly all three of them were kneeling on the floor at once, giving me hugs, telling me everything would be okay, speaking to me soothingly while quietly sending recriminating words back and forth which I heard snatches of, like my Mom to Patrice: "This is all your fault, you slut."

And Ellie: "Who has been helping this girl with her legal problems? Who? We have a talented woman here who could make a fortune with a little help..."

Patrice: "I came over, which I felt was very brave..."

Mom to Patrice: "Oh my God, I forgot to say congratulations on your uncle being named French ambassador! I came over to show Carly the picture of you in the Post, actually."

Ellie to Patrice: "Will he be selling his current home?"

Patrice (defiant; loved that about her) to all of us: "If you'd listen to what really happened, you would never believe it. You'd say 'I am so sorry' to me a thousand times." Her hands waved around, gesturing. "I'm here to give you valuable information that will change everything in your favor. *That* is why I am here." Then proud and a bit huffy, "I did not have to come, you know."

Everyone nodded in agreement.

Ellie to Mom: "Open the folder and let's see the contract."

Mom did, although I know she was much more interested in what Patrice had to say.

There was another knock at the door, and Mom turned automatically and opened it as the papers spread all over the kitchen floor. Alex slipped in and immediately bent over to help pick up the contract.

"Oh, shit." Ellie bent down to help. In the chaos, Patrice leaned down and whispered to me, "I have something for you. Come with me." She dragged me off the floor and led me into the living room, then decided that wasn't private enough and pushed me upstairs to my bedroom, where I collapsed onto the bed. She closed the door and lay next to me. We stared at the ceiling.

"Oh, Patrice."

"Oh, Carly." We both sighed, saddened beyond words at our loss.

She handed me two papers. One named Paul Macalister as being suspended from U.S. Air for three months for the consumption of alcohol in a Miami motel room less than twelve hours before flying, as well as a citation for disorderly conduct. It was dated October 21st.

The next piece of paper was a copy of an arrest report dated December 23rd at 2:00 a.m. That was the night (or technically the next day) when Patrice and Paul had spent the night at the Doubletree. That was all a lie?

"Your husband threatened to have me deported on the next flight back to France if I didn't cover for him. And I felt guilty as well, since if I hadn't wanted to go to Georgetown so much he wouldn't have insisted on driving me." She paused. "But I didn't think he'd stay with us and go dancing. It was so embarrassing. Finally I left him there and went home with my cousins."

"You didn't fuck him?" I felt so detached from the situation that I could have been on another planet.

Patrice bolted upright. "What are you saying? I would not get near that man if…Is that what he told you? Mrs. Carly, come ON! No disrespect, but he is disgusting. He followed me all night and after I had left for my cousins' home, your husband called my cell phone as his one-and-only call, and if it had not been for my family, Paul Macalister would have stayed right in jail. I wish I had left him there."

Patrice's long dark hair had turned blonde. Her make-up was more subtle and much more expensive than when she was a fresh young girl arriving from France with glitter in her eyes.

Her wool light summer suit with a black hat and white rim made her look as though she was going to the White House for lunch. How the hell had she done all of this? I wondered briefly. And the limo!

But Patrice's expression when she was animated was the same Patrice I adored. Her passion showed in her eyes as it always had. Still, she looked older to me. Sophistication does that. Or maybe I was jealous. I still shopped at Marshall's.

"And then Paul turned nasty," she told me slowly, like a climax of a horror story. "He intimidated me." Maybe she spent all her money to put on a show for me. "Paul convinced me that if I told one word of this to you I would be deported. Remember, he had all my working papers, the contract of my employment, my passport, my work visa, and many of my other things all locked up in his desk. One mention of any of this to you and I was out of the country, never to return. This is what he told me over and over again. Didn't you see that?"

My mind was a little bit in disarray. The porch, the party, Alex, John, Naomi, the mess, the house for sale, everyone over at my house, and now Patrice taking my assumptions and what I believed to be the truth and turning it all upside down?

Patrice stood up all flushed and folded her arms (which was another of her gestures that endeared her to me). "Well?" she demanded, either furious or a brilliant actress. Without thinking she started picking up my clothes, sorting them into piles…"I could only tell you today because I now have amnesty due to the fact that my uncle is officially the French ambassador. You know, Paul made me so angry with you. I did my best to forget about you and the whole horrible experience. But I could never forget you. Your husband is a very, very, evil man."

She planted my undies in the laundry basket.

I shot up from the bed and shouted, "You fucked him at the Doubletree! You wanted to go to the Ritz!"

"That's a lie!" she shouted right back. I grabbed her and she grabbed me and we shouted and fought and clawed each other, screaming:

Me: "You had all those fancy clothes, you whore."

Patrice: "I came from money! My clothes—my *possessions*—are none of your business!"

Me: "Paul got them for you. You tricked me."

Patrice: "You are insane. Most of my clothes have always been at my family's house. Those things were practically nothing. Your disgusting husband has never touched me and has never bought me even a metro pass."

I stopped fighting. So every time Paul dropped Patrice at the metro and assured me he had taken care of a tip, money for the metro, money in case she got in trouble, he was lying? Why? There was no reason. "Liar!" I attacked her again.

"I wasn't even paid the last three weeks I worked. Look at this paper." Patrice crammed it into my face. "Your husband was arrested leaving Georgetown that night. We got him out of jail the next morning. He came back to the house, took a shower, and even borrowed my uncle's suit. He asked for privacy to call you, and George, my cousin, led him into the library. All he told us was that he did not want to upset you, so he told you that he had spent the night at the Doubletree (she made a huge face) and he asked us to back him up. A minor white lie, he said. My cousins and uncle understood perfectly. We even fed him lunch." She paused. Then she became enraged again. "He never wanted you to know and he got meaner and meaner to me. Are you blind or crazy?" Patrice collapsed and seemed to have trouble breathing. "The clock!"

"Calm down. It's okay. I believe you."

"And to think when we came back the next afternoon," Patrice continued between sobs, "I thought everything would be fine." She could barely speak. "And you crushed my favorite clock my brother gave me when I was six!"

Now the girl was hysterical. She was crying so loud I thought the people downstairs might suspect I was murdering her.

"I'll get you a new one," I assured her. She started howling. "I'll pay your brother and *he* can get you a new one," I told her gently, kind of alarmed at her reaction about the loss of a simple alarm clock. Personally, I hate alarm—

"HE'S DEAD!"

I literally fell back from her body in shock.

Patrice and I managed to crawl back onto the bed where the tears just flowed from both of us. Our abrupt parting, the betrayal, the pain, the lies, the fact that we had both lost our brothers, the misunderstandings, and the hurt over everything was just too much. She was part of my family. She had thought she was.

We'd blocked within ourselves how much we missed each other. How much we had missed. How could someone I was married to do this to me? To the kids? To Patrice? How?

"He is the father of my children."

"Neither one of them are anything like him," she replied.

We lay next to each other on the bed for twenty minutes or so. I wanted to ask her about her brother, her life since she left, how Paul had threatened her, how sorry I was, how I had looked for her, how much I had missed her.

"There is much for both of us to say." Patrice had read my thoughts. "We'll have plenty of time." She took my hand and squeezed it. "I'm the deputy spokesperson for the French embassy. We'll see each other a great deal."

"Quite a step up!" I chirped.

Patrice smiled. "That's for sure, but I miss it here as well."

Suddenly I heard my father's voice downstairs and so did Patrice. We both scrambled off the bed automatically and ran down the stairs. My father? He never got involved in messy things! He'd done enough of that at the CIA. No, that wasn't it. He just couldn't bear personal injury when it came to me after Timmy died. That was up to Mom.

Patrice and I entered the kitchen. We must have looked like quite a pair.

My father was all business. "Patrice, I understand you may have some evidence that could help us in this unfortunate situation."

She handed Dad her two pieces of paper. "These are copies," she told him meekly. "I would have told you before but..."

Dad put his hand up. "I understand, Patrice. It's fine. You were a victim too."

How did he know so much?

Dad read the papers in less than a second. "Very good." Dad and Alex turned and left. They were definitely on a mission.

"Well," Ellie said with fake bravado, "I need to get back to work, but this has been an interesting morning and, Carly, you have been very brave and you are lucky to have these people who love you." She came over to me and gave me a quick hug and kiss and she was gone.

"She's not used to these things," Mom said to no one in particular in her off-handed way.

Patrice was next. She gave Mom a hug and then me. "I can't keep the driver all day." We laughed. Then I scrambled for my purse and emptied it out on the floor.

"You don't have a wallet?" Patrice asked, teasing.

"I do, but I always forget to put things in it."

The three of us smiled.

I was shuffling through my money to pay Patrice for the month that my loser husband had not paid her when Patrice firmly dragged me back upright. "You can give it to me in person another time. Let's make a date. I know: the very day I get back from Paris!"

"Good, we have a date," I told Patrice. The tears were coming. "I'm giving a rabbit funeral tonight and I'd love you to come."

"Jake?" she asked.

I nodded solemnly. We both started laughing and she gave me another huge hug. "Oh, Carly, that's hysterical. A rabbit funeral. Hah!" Patrice looked torn for a moment. "I would love it, but I leave for Paris tonight."

"Don't worry. I'm sure there'll be others." Mom quipped.

I glared at her.

"No more rabbits," Patrice and I said together like we used to, since we always joked about what a pain it was feeding and cleaning out Jake's cage, only to force him outside for a little R and R and he'd sit there like a statue.

"Gee, Paris or a party at Carly's?" I pretended I was deciding.

Patrice smiled. Suddenly she grabbed Mom and me by the shoulders. "Next time, I bring you. A promise. We're going to Paris!" She was clapping, jumping up and down.

"I have a free trip to Paris and I'm taking Carly since her father won't leave the garage now that he has that new effing truck. Anyway, so we'll work it all out!" Mom was breathless.

Patrice hugged her again. "Of course! You were born for Paris." Then Patrice reached into her impeccable Gucci and retrieved her calendar book. She studied it intently and looked up.

"April seventh through the twenty-second would work beautifully. You can stay at my family's palace (Patrice looked embarrassed for a moment but recovered as if she had decided, "What the hell? My family owns a palace"), and it is gorgeous in April. We'll have a tremendous party. You'll meet everyone!" That was it. "I'm planning everything," she continued, acting very French.

"It's the kids' vacation." My stomach dropped. Paul would never take them for ten days.

"I know. That's why I chose those dates." She had to be joking. "We have to bring Kerry and Jamie! They would adore all my nieces and nephews and there are many servants, so it won't be a burden on you." She gave me this pleading look. Like I was going to say "no."

Patrice and Mom reminded me—not that this was on my mind or anything—of bunnies. Bunnies have great PR. We think of them as hopping all around, enthusiastic and curious about their world, and so cute they could endear themselves to anyone. The Easter bunny and the Playboy bunny helped their reputation. Anyway, between Mom and Patrice, the excitement in the air was so strong I thought Mom might float right up through the roof. Patrice was barely out the door when Mom leapt up from her chair, clapping her hands and swirling around the kitchen.

"A palace! Oh my Lord, Carly. We will have the time of our *lives;* do you know how different the French are? They *enjoy* life. They love clothes, fabulous food, beautiful smells, and exotic parties. It's incredible." Dad and Mom had gone there once and told us it was the best time of their lives. "I thought we were the best time of your lives," Timmy had teased her.

"No wonder they hate most Americans. We are so boring, it's unspeakable." Mom shuddered. "I have to start getting ready."

"It's July." I knew I'd be getting ready April 6th.

Mom was onto a new thought. "And I know for a fact Patrice will invite us to all those legendary French embassy parties when she's in Washington. Do you know how absolutely fabulous the French embassy is, Carly? Your father and I used to go there all the time." A shadow crossed Mom's face. She brushed it away. "For God's sake, Carly, you have six hours before your party! I'm calling Naomi. By the way, Alex calmly explained to each and every agent that the listing has been canceled indefinitely. Then he cleaned the porch as much as he could and drove your father downtown with the papers to see your lawyer."

"Wow!" I was touched and shocked.

"You have to appreciate those who love you," Mom lectured, meaning *her*.

"Mom, are you Jewish?"

"Don't you start with that Jewish mother crap. You sound just like Timmy."

She was at the door. I didn't want her to leave. She looked up at me. "Well, start getting ready! I want you to look like an angel tonight. A shining star! Go get a manicure and have that mop on your head cleaned up."

I promised her I would.

FIFTEEN

Mom and Dad were the hit of what turned out to be a very wild party. You know how funerals are—everyone drinks too much, gets emotional, talks about how short life is, and recounts stories about various loved ones. My father brought over the Best of Frank Sinatra and Cole Porter, and all my friends ended up coming because they had nothing else to do, so it was quite a scene. The trick is to serve incredibly deadly rum drinks at the very beginning of the party, around six o'clock, to loosen things up.

The party was outdoors and very crowded and I didn't see Alex arrive. Both John and Alex were coming, but I couldn't worry about that. Anyway, John was going to be late due to a mandatory annual meeting in his office where they announced the next year's partners, and I think he'd been waiting for this chance since before he was born. That's all he talked about. And he worked late every night and all weekend when he wasn't with me. Maybe that's why he was so wild when he had a break. Moderation would be a good word for John and me to learn.

After greeting the guests, making sure they had a cocktail, supervising Jamie and Kerry passing the appetizers, I suddenly spotted Alex. He was talking to my parents with an Extremely Attractive Nymphet at his side. Mother, who has had this incredibly accurate homing device for my location since I was a child, spotted me and waved with both hands, making me want to sink in horror.

"Oh, Carly," she called out, hands cupped so it would be really loud, "don't just dawdle at the bar. Come *over* here." Yes, Mother Dear. I was not dawdling at the bar.

As I approached, I heard Mom tell the group, "Actually, I have one very special angel. Her name is Catriona. Isn't that beautiful? It's much more interesting than Catherine. But I had no choice in the matter," she laughed. She named me Catherine.

"You did with me," I reminded her; suddenly angry she'd told everyone my name was boring.

"Really?" Naive Nymphet asked my mom, ignoring me. "Does this angel guide you in any way?"

"Carly, I want you to meet Lucy," Mom quickly introduced us. Lucy-nymph said hello to me briefly and turned her attention back to Mom. Apparently Lucy was fascinated with angels.

"Of course. I consult her about everything. We have our fights, but that's normal when you are so close, you see."

"Quite a funeral," Alex said to me, looking around. "The rabbit would be honored."

I noticed some of the guests clearing away all the debris and making what was left of the porch into a dance floor. The Macarena had just started playing (Mom's request – mortifying) but everyone immediately began forming lines, while Tina, who can be bossy at times, yelled directions.

"Cute date," I told Alex.

"Carly likes to keep her a secret. She doesn't believe the way I do, you see," Mom was informing a captivated Lucy. "But, truly, it's like this angel has a computer line directly to God."

"She's not a real date," Alex told me.

Mom turned her attention to us. "Oh Carly, come *on*. Tell Lucinda here about how much my angel has helped us."

Us?

There was an expectant silence.

Finally I said, "I...I think Mom's angel *talks* to angels, I'm not sure if she is one herself."

Mom looked crushed. "But of course she really is. Absolutely."

No one said anything. I turned to Alex. "What's the difference between real and not real?"

"How profound," exclaimed the nineteen-year-old-nymphet, assuming we were talking about angels.

"It's confusing," he admitted.

"Let's dance," exclaimed Lucy, turning to Alex.

"No," said Alex to Lucy, his eyes in mine. "We should probably make it an early night."

"That would make it worse," I said.

"Are we going to dance or not?" demanded Lucy.

"Of course you should!" I said cheerily and walked away my best mysterious, aloof, and false self. I pretended to be having a great time. I talked and laughed with all the other guests. What was my problem? Was I so demented that just because John was still a no-show I immediately became jealous of Alex even though I knew because he *told* me in so many words that I would never ever make him happy? I had the nerve to act like a two-year-old and be upset just because he brought a date. I should get my money back from Knot, I thought, since I was worse instead of better.

I headed into the house for a little reality check. Good thing. Naomi, from Sri Lanka, whom Mom hired for me as a present to cook the dinner, was standing at the kitchen stove, looking perplexed. I went over to her. She was hovering over a huge pot of boiling water that had five cans of tuna fish in it. I didn't understand what she was doing, since the cans weren't opened.

"Cook! I no cook." She was firm.

"What do you mean, 'you no cook?'"

"Clean, Madam."

I panicked. "But Mom said..."

"No more. Too old. Tired of cooking."

"Oh shit."

I raced outside, flying past John as he grabbed my arm and swirled me around. "Carly, what's wrong? Is the house on fire?"

Should I tell him? He might think it was odd. "Nothing!" I chirped, and tried to loosen my arm to go tell my mother that the woman she hired was a freak. But John led me firmly back into the house while I explained to him, in tears, that this Naomi woman, who was supposed to make the entire dinner, had come to the untimely conclusion that she really did not and would not cook after all.

John held me to him, whispering in my ear (which made me want to ravage him on the spot), "Carly Macalister. What in the world am I going to do with you?" And then he gave me this deep, penetrating, no-nonsense kiss and his hand was slipping down my back, his other was in my hair, and my lower body was leaning forward toward him.

Where the hell is a private bedroom? I wondered.

"I'm partner," he whispered.

"Oh my God, John, that's fantastic!"

"Let's sneak into the den."

"Can't yet, no dinner, remember?"

And then John went into action. He paged the caterer that worked for his firm and less than an hour later the Mexican delight of the century was being served outside to all the guests, who gobbled it down since they were most likely starving by that point, when really good decadent food is like heaven.

My hero. I watched John laugh and mingle with the guests and then walked back to the kitchen where I checked to see if Naomi was doing *anything*, such as cleaning up. She was watching television, but I couldn't worry about it.

"Take me to bed," I thought, observing John through the bathroom window with the lights off so no one could see me. He moved effortlessly from table to table between the guests to make sure everyone was happy.

I walked down from the kitchen toward him, smiling, concentrating on walking with sex appeal like in commercials.

Suddenly my high heel sank into the ground and I hurled forward straight into the muddy grass. I looked up and there was Paul.

"Okay," I thought to myself, "disentangle brand new high heel shoe from mud. Wipe mud from eye and hope you are seeing things. Get up slowly so that black sheer shirt does not reveal breast. Stand and look around."

Mom and Dad looked like they had been shot. No one moved. "This is definitely a dream," I thought. "No more rum drinks." Unfortunately, I had been too busy to drink them and Paul was, indeed, standing in front of me.

"You look wonderful, Carly, just wonderful." His iciest voice and smile chilled me like they always had. "Here is the settlement, Carly, baby."

I glanced at Dad. He gave me a signal, like, "don't do anything."

Paul was the one who was drunk. He leaned toward me and I thought he might push me down again. But he whispered in my ear, as sarcastically as possible, "Sorry I lied to you about everything. It was so much fun while it lasted." And he handed me the package. Had he signed it or not? I wanted to tear it open right then and there. It only held my entire future in it. Had he signed or was he going to fight me in court, costing me a fortune that I didn't have, which would mean I would have to give in?

Not a soul moved, wondering what he was saying or what he was going to do. Were we in a play? Why the hell had the music stopped? Oh, right, I asked them to refrain during dinner.

Did he sign our counterproposal or not? We had proof against him. I bet he did. Had I won? Nobody wins, I remembered. The kids had no real father anymore, I was a single mother, money would always be hard, Christmas and birthdays would always be split up and affect Jamie and Kerry forever, and he'd lied to me over and over again to make me feel like a useless piece of shit. I had married one of the cruelest, cheating liars and shared my life with him for fifteen years. And now he was at my party, ruining it, making a scene, humiliating me, drunk and pathetic, attempting to hurt me as much as possible again. But it was my choice—I could be immune to his poison. "Pretend you're Katherine Hepburn in a showdown," I thought.

"Lynch him!" I yelled at the top of my voice and started to laugh. "Just kidding." I kept chuckling and so did some others, trying to grasp the moment. "Everyone say, 'bye bye, Paul.'"

Alex, Dad, and Tina, along with everyone else at the party, moved a little closer to him, subconsciously protecting me in case he decided to go for my throat or something. "Bye, Paul!" I yelled in a fake cheerful voice, waving my hand like first ladies do. He looked around, got nervous, turned and made a hasty exit, slinking like the snake that he was back under the rock from which he came.

I waved to everyone, "That was my surprise entertainment for this evening. And now, I'm going to change. Let's get the music back!" I hobbled into the house, tossed off the muddy shoes, and ran up to my bedroom. Package or shower first? I was wondering when John knocked and walked in before I had moved.

"Jesus. You have the most guts of any woman on earth." He came up and kissed my mud and me. "I think you look arousing just like you are." Yum. "Very primitive, like Jane." He engulfed me. Steering me toward the bed. I was laughing, trying to protest, "John, I'm having a party, you bad boy." Plop. Mud all over the place.

"I'll be good. Just wanted to tell you a secret."

"You don't have to whisper. We're the only ones here."

"Well, since I made partner today, I bought you a little…" He fumbled around in his pocket. "Don't get scared, it's not a ring." We both stood up and he handed me a velvet box.

"I love it. I love velvet boxes! Thank you so much!" I gave him a huge hug.

"Open it, you wacko."

"John, I want to do it with you and take my time." I paused. "I'll get rid of everyone and you stay, okay? I'll make the kids go to Mom and Dad's." John smiled. "They'll be asleep so they won't know the difference. And since it's Friday night, it's fine. Now get the hell out of here so I can change!"

"Carly, are you coming?" Mom was wriggling the locked doorknob.

John and I looked at each other. "Right down, Mom."

"Okay, but—"

"One sec."

We heard Mom leaving. "Go!" I ordered John. I ran into the bathroom, hopped in the shower and dried off, all in about two minutes, singing something, on top of the world, thinking deranged thoughts like, "That'll teach Alex when I stay with John, serves him right for bringing that slut to my house." Was Alex trying to make me jealous? Get even? Of course he was. Showing me that at the snap of a finger he could bring a gorgeous, sexy, tiny thing to my house who absolutely seemed to revere the ground he walked on. Well, I would be having just a fine time with John and I'd make sure Alex knew it.

I came back into my room and stopped. John was sitting on my bed. Next to him was the un-opened settlement package. His face looked like grey plaster.

"What's wrong?" I asked, annoyed that he hadn't gone back down to the party so I could tear the package open and look for Paul's signature of acceptance. I didn't want anyone with me when I looked. It was too personal. However it went, I'd tell John about it later. And I was in a huge hurry.

"Shit. Oh my God. This is crazy. This is absurd. Jesus Christ." I had never even heard John swear hardly at all. What could be so wrong with *him?* He wasn't the one going through any of this. John leaned down with his elbows on his knees and his hands rubbing the sides of his head while I was tearing through my dresser, hopping on one leg, than the other, throwing on panties, grabbing a bra, fluttering around for a shirt.

"Fuck. I cannot believe this," he moaned.

I became impatient and a little concerned because he seemed to be having an anxiety attack. When John sat up he was all sweaty in the face, his hands were shaking, and he was moaning and mumbling, "Great, just great." Over and over.

"What the hell is wrong?" I asked with a touch of anger, pouring into some jeans. I had about fifty guests downstairs,

I hadn't eaten dinner or had one drink, or spent time with anyone, and they probably thought I'd jumped out of the window at this point and it was rude. "Tell me. I've got to get back to the party right this second, John. This is rude."

"Your husband hired our firm to represent him."

I felt stone cold. "Excuse me?"

He held up the package.

"Swartz, Reilly, and West," I read.

"And Davenport after today."

And Davenport after today.

"Bittersweet, I would say," John mumbled with an ironic, sad smile. He stood up from the bed and spoke slowly, refusing to look me in the eye. "And so now, as a partner of the firm, all cases are my business. But I promise you nothing that happened between us in the past is evidence or relevant in any way to this case and will never be disclosed to anyone." That hadn't even crossed my mind. So what if a woman wants some nooky while the philandering, cheating son-of-a-bitch concedes to taking the children for a day or two? Whose business was that? I wasn't harming anyone.

"What the hell does that mean? I did nothing wrong." Anger was rising to my cheeks. It's not like John told me gently, "As soon as you're settlement is reached it won't matter, so it's just a little time, right?" Or "I loved being with you, Carly, I can't believe this, we'll think of something," or "I'll just look for another firm if that's what it takes." No. This was a dump.

"Just leave, John." I couldn't look at him.

"So it would be impossible for us to continue." John wanted to make sure I understood.

"Leave now."

"Yes, right, I understand." He placed a piece of paper on my desk. Maybe it said, "Just kidding. Love you."

I walked over and studied it.

"The bill for dinner," he explained, "like we discussed. I think it's quite reasonable."

"Yes. Thank you."

"I think it would be appropriate if you gave me the present back."

John backed out of my room as I approached him. When we got to the door, he got more nervous, knowing I could shove him right down the stairs.

"Trespassing and, let's see, inappropriate sexual advances should do it. Oops. Beloved career gone. Now get out of my house."

John turned and fled down the stairs and out the door.

I slammed the bedroom door, grabbed the vase I made in third grade, and shattered it against the mirror just like in the movies.

"What the hell are you doing?" Tina was pounding and screaming at the door and marching in at the same time. "Oh shit, you're having a breakdown. Don't worry, the party's in full swing and not a soul's missed you. That band is sooo good. Cheer up!" She grabbed my purse and dumped it on the carpet, searching for make-up. She sorted it all from the other junk.

"We can't talk about whatever is wrong now since there's no time and we can both cry later. So put it all out of your mind because you've got to get back out there, right?"

I nodded.

"Where's John?" Tina asked from the bathroom where she was wetting a cloth. She started drying off my red, puffy eyes and cheeks. My dear, sweet, reliable, best friend in the world Tina. I started sobbing in earnest as Tina wiped more frantically, saying, "Men? If you are crying about a man then I'm going to slap you. I told you they are worthless. Just use them." She spotted the velvet box on the floor and looked up at me. I nodded and she tore it open.

"It was from John right before he dumped me and then he wanted to take it back." The short version.

"Over my dead body, the cheap shit, you're keeping it." Inside were sterling silver earrings with a green stone at the end. We stared at each other.

"Emeralds?" we asked at once.

"Put them on. You look gorgeous. Promise. Next…" She picked up the settlement package. "Should we open it?" I nodded. Tina tore it apart like a tigress eating her dinner. She skimmed it and broke into a wallop with her fist in the air and I knew. Everything was going to be just fine.

Especially when you have a friend like Tina.

Alex was walking down the lawn from the kitchen as Tina closed the kitchen door behind us. Had he come to see me and chickened out? I had no idea why I should care if he brought a beautiful date to my party. It was just that, if he really fell in love with her, I would lose him, because I had hated the girl instantly. And I really didn't want to lose Alex because he'd been steady as a rock for me my entire adult life and, in fact, my childhood as well. If he married, for instance, he'd be gone. It always happens. Friends promise and swear they will be different and they can still go with you to Austin Grill at the drop of a hat, but they don't.

We crept across the lawn and strolled up to the bar like I had been at the party all along and asked for champagne.

"Do I look okay?" I asked Tina.

"Fantastic. You have that mysterious, alluring look. I can't get that."

"Hey, you look like the Queen of Rock, baby." Tina was dressed in the purple mini-skirt I gave her for Christmas, the sweet thing, and she looked beautiful, although maybe slightly out of season, since it was suede. She had her black boots on and her hair was freshly colored, I'd have to say, purple. Her hazel eyes always shone like a full moon.

I held up the champagne glass. "I'm going to drink this every night for the rest of my life."

"I think you look gorgeous too," added the bartender, Sean. He was about twenty-five.

I smiled. "It's not tip time yet."

Tina slapped me lightly on my arm. "Jesus, Carly, learn to take a compliment."

"Oh! Thank you so much, Sean. What are you doing later?"

The three of us laughed.

"Don't think it hasn't crossed my mind," Sean responded, and I smiled. He was flirting with me. How adorable.

Tina dragged me toward the group. "I fucked him," she whispered as we walked across the lawn. "Fabulous. Built like a horse."

Mother was having a ball—dancing a bit and talking to everyone as her spirits lifted higher and became lighter, as if she lit up the entire party. It was this gift that made me love her so much my heart ached watching her. Dad was having a fine time as well, cornering a group of Alex's friends (doctors) to discuss his various ailments in detail. Tina grabbed Phil the contractor's hand and suddenly she was dancing a bit wild on the dance floor and I was standing there alone.

Alex had his arm around Lucy, talking to a group of various acquaintances of mine. Alex turned and saw me alone. I looked away, embarrassed.

If Alex liked girls like this Lucinda woman/child, I must have been overestimating him. She did have thick blonde hair, but so did I—and mine was real. Her make-up was so thick I could chip it off her face with a palette knife. Her clothes were impeccable, but she'd definitely be high maintenance. Fine, if that's the type he wanted, he could have her. Lucinda was deeply involved in some conversation, maybe about Dr. Seuss.

Alex excused himself and started toward me as I warded off all feelings of hurt and confusion, of sadness and doubt. The music stopped and Tina hunted the crowd for me, but she saw Alex next to me and didn't approach. The band changed to Frank. He led me to dance. We always danced. It was no big deal. But to our favorite song? I wondered vaguely if he had requested it. No, Carly, *he's with someone else.*

It was a slow dance. His arm around mine made my arm shiver. He held me closer. I didn't have to do a thing: Alex had always been the best dancer in the world.

We were the only ones dancing.

"Fly me to the moon…"

Hold me close. Hold me.

"Are you okay?" Alex asked.

"And let me play among the stars" "WHAT DO YOU MEAN, AM I OKAY?? Am I okay that you are on a date? That John left me without even a hug goodbye? That I've always loved you and you're with another girl? John was my practice, you idiot."

"Not exactly." My voice sounded shaky.

Alex swirled me around. He kissed me softly, slowly on the cheek.

"Let me see what life is like on Jupiter and Mars"

I held him as tight as I could, my face buried in his jacket. "You never bring your girls here. It must be serious," I whispered.

"In other words, hold my hand"

"Not me." He lifted my head to his cheek. "I don't fall that fast," he whispered, alluding to John.

"I know what I'm doing." I said quickly, defensive, lying. Why??

"In other words, baby, kiss me..."

I could feel his breath. I could feel everything. I felt like I might cry. "Actually, that's not true, Alex, and you know it. You've always known."

"I'm happy for you, Carly. You just dove right in." I *had* hurt him. Shit.

"In other words, please be true..."

"No! I don't feel like that at all! He doesn't mean—"

"You should go for it," he interrupted. Another twirl. I felt sick.

We stopped dancing. "Is that what you really want me to do?

"Perhaps it would be best." His tone was even. He wore no readable expression. So I turned to walk away. He didn't stop me.

"In other words, I (Bam) LOVE (Bam) YOU!"

SIXTEEN

Tina woke me the next morning. She'd spent the night because I begged her to. She hopped right up on my bed.

"Okay, I have come to a brilliant conclusion. I should probably be a philosopher or something."

"Yes?" I was waiting.

"I think the best thing we could do is date a lot of men and not have sex with any of them."

"That sounds good," I told her.

"There are just two difficulties: finding the men and not having the sex."

I was trying really hard not to think about sex and men after the rabbit funeral fiasco with the rejection of two (three, actually, if you included Paul) men in one evening. Still, for a while, say fifteen minutes or so, being an eternal optimist and always believing in new beginnings, I had this tremendous feeling that everything was going to be wonderful. Perhaps this was partly due to the new anti-depressant Dr. Knot thought I might enjoy. I had taken my very first pill right when I woke up this morning. I suspected it might have been a placebo, which, according to the studies, worked just as well as the real thing. It's the same principle as believing the horoscopes from the newspaper. They never say anything too frightening like, "watch out, today will be horribly depressing as well as danger-ous." Or "Your husband will leave you today and you will be all alone and extremely poor." Or "Today you will go to the doctor and find out you have a fatal blood disease." They never say things like that, and yet these things happen to people all the time.

You'd think the phone call from my lawyer would have cheered me up. She called to congratulate me and inform me my copy of the agreement was in the mail. I didn't want to take her thunder and tell her I already knew. Paul had agreed to sign it since he had lied about his arrest, hid pertinent facts regard-ing his employment, and *blackmailed a member of the French ambassador's family.* That was the turning point, the lawyer told me. Paul thought they might drag him back to France and guil-lotine him.

But the crème-de-la-crème was: my father's and mine were the only names the contract had listed under "Purchaser" since my father had put up the down payment (Dad thought it was an excellent investment and he was right) and Dad had the loan for the first year. I never knew any of this. I had been really young, living in dead Timmy shock, and against the idea of moving into a house in the first place. I had no clue what I was doing, which was probably why I married the very first person I met after Timmy died. Paul and Dad had a separate agreement about the payback, but Paul apparently never honored it and Dad never brought it up to me. So Dad and I had made a very good investment and I never even knew it. Paul didn't own an inch of this house.

Then the lawyer said goodbye/good luck and hung up. Typical lawyer—all nice to you in the beginning so they can take your money or get in your pants and then they are gone.

I couldn't dwell on anything—good or bad, which was a blessing, actually, since I was frantically packing the kids for their month with their beloved father when I realized he had signed it because then he'd come over and murder me. Paul was coming to pick up the kids and drive them to his parents' farm in New Hampshire for the month of July as pre-arranged. I put 911 on speed dial just in case.

Finally Jamie and Kerry's suitcases were closed and out the door and all of their keep-busy-in-the-car stuff were in their backpacks.

The kids waited for their father on the kitchen stoop for nearly an hour—two days in kid time. I kept taking them cookies and lemonade to distract them. They had dressed themselves. Kerry looked like she was going to church—blonde hair combed back neatly in a barrette, black buckled shoes, and the most adorable gingham dress I had ever seen. (Mom had given it to her.) Jamie looked like he was going to a rap concert. He had the mandatory backwards baseball hat, the extra-long and three-sizes-too-large shorts with the chain belt, and tennis shoes with no laces. It was hard to believe they were from the same family. Sometimes it was hard to comprehend that they were my children. I felt overwhelmed with sadness that they'd be gone so long, like I was being stabbed.

Kerry handled her father's tardiness by calmly coloring with one hand and clutching the handle of her pink plastic suitcase with the other. She refused to use any other suitcase. Jamie, on the other hand, appeared at first restless, then anxious, then frustrated, then angry. He picked up his duffle bag and started kicking it around like a soccer ball. It made *me* frustrated and angry to see him go through this. Why can't a person show up when he says he will? I went outside and sat with them for a few minutes.

"Mom, if he sees you he'll get in a bad mood," Jamie told me.

"I'm leaving. I just wanted to say hi."

"Hi," said Kerry.

"Why couldn't he get here in time for my game?" asked Jamie, who'd had his final league soccer game two hours earlier.

Because your father's a selfish child, I wanted to say.

"Where is he, anyway?" Jamie continued, squirming around and chewing on a hangnail.

"Don't chew your fingernails," I snapped at him. Everyone was tense.

Finally Paul arrived, plopping down in a chair in the kitchen before I could say no. I told him the kids had been waiting over an hour for his arrival, so perhaps he should get on the road, but Paul insisted that he needed to talk to me, so they went outside to wait some more.

"What?" I was impatient.

He looked around and back at me. "You look wonderful, Carly." He sighed. "I gave up a lot, didn't I?"

"Just your family, no big deal."

"Are you happy, Carly? I mean, maybe we should reconsider this." Feeling poor, asshole? Missing the house you wanted to take away from me? I didn't want any confrontations. I was sick of them.

"Jesus, Paul, don't you think it's a little late?"

He stood and came close. He was making me sick. I wanted to tell him he was disgusting.

"The single life gets old, you know?" His face was reddish and crusty and his eyes, slightly bloodshot, looked blank.

His stomach protruded over his jeans, which made his body seem out of proportion.

"Well, there's Dawn, then."

"I don't love her or any of them. You know I loved you, right?" He moved closer. I could feel his small soul, and the meanness that always kept me at bay. I thought I was going to be sick. He was such a good liar. I had to give him that.

I took a step back. "I am the happiest I've ever been because I don't have to live with you."

He laughed. "Sure, you're a real catch. The guys are swarming after you."

I turned like I'd been slapped but he couldn't see the hurt. How could I still let him get to me? Kerry and Jamie came back inside, looking at both of us with imploring eyes.

"We've been waiting for about a year," Kerry informed us politely.

Paul wandered around the kitchen. I didn't know what he was thinking. I think he always believed I'd take him back. I was a "reserve" to come back to when he got tired of it all. No, that wasn't it. He wanted to get me to say "yes" so he could say "no," because he got his kicks from hurting other people. That was exactly it. Game over.

I sauntered up to him, smiling, and whispered in his ear, "Get out of my fucking house, asshole, before I call the police. You're making me sick." Then I turned quickly and picked Kerry up.

"I know, and you guys have had to wait way too long, but you're going right this second. Promise!"

I practically pushed Paul outside, walked the kids to the car, and hugged them both really tight. Then I handed them each their backpacks and walked away before I had time to say something that would make it all harder.

I watched them drive down the driveway from the kitchen window. It was like my life was leaving in a tiny, vulnerable car all together, without me.

SEVENTEEN

Alex finally called and left a message. It was typical Alex. "Hi. It's me. We're all meeting down on the Potomac at eight-thirty Sunday night for a mid-summer cookout. Bring some wine and wood." He can be *so* romantic. Who is "We're all?" And where on the Potomac? I could see myself traipsing all around Washington, combing the parks and going up to cook-outs with people huddled around them only to realize I didn't know a soul because it wasn't the right party, and then apologizing and backing away in the darkness like some lunatic.

But actually, Alex was just being sweet because he'd know how hard it would be for me to let my children leave with the only person on earth that I had to try and pray about so I wouldn't be filled with hatred for him. And the longest I'd been away from them was the week at Christmas. Still, I was mad at Alex too. So I called Tina instead, and we decided to go to Austin Grill to gobble down nachos and celebrate our freedom.

"I can't believe it! There's that asshole!" Tina was all flushed.

"Which one?" I asked. And then I turned around and it was one of her musician clients. His name was Jack. Tina always got emotionally involved with her clients. "Don't worry, he's leaving. Don't stare. Act detached. Ignore him," I instructed.

"When you think about all that useless time I spent trying to help that selfish brat move into his house. God! And he treats me like—"

"He didn't ask you to help him. You offered," I pointed out.

"He acts like we're friends or something. It's completely humiliating."

"Forget him," I told her firmly.

"Try taking your own advice."

"Alex is history. I've moved on," I announced. Then, since she appeared to be sinking into a severe depression because the Jack creature left the bar, I tried to take her mind off of it by admitting to a silly little plan I had made.

"That's crazy. Why didn't you tell me?"

"I knew you'd be judgmental. I hate that."

"I'm never judgmental. But make a reservation at the Ritz so you can ask Alex over for a drink?"

"I cancelled the reservation five minutes later. It was just to win him back after the rabbit funeral." Very childish move, I had to admit. "You see how judgmental you are? See?" She was making it worse.

"This Alex problem has got to be fixed. I thought Dr. Shrink was helping you with this."

"I'm working on it as we speak."

She kept staring at me. "I don't think he's helping."

"I'm getting much better." I folded my arms. Tina was acting as if she were perfect, which was extremely annoying. "At least I didn't sleep with my sex therapist!" I blurted out. Everyone in the restaurant heard. Thank God Jack had just left. Tina's face started getting puffy. "We're practicing lines for a play," I announced to the room.

Tina was hissing at me, "He was not *my* sex therapist. He was *a* sex therapist and there's a big difference!"

"I don't care. Two men walk into a bar and announce that they're sex therapists and you tell them all about your sex life and then you end up sleeping with one?" I hissed back.

"Two months later! You act like it was a one night stand." The whole place was silent.

"I just want you to know I'm not the only crazy one around here," I announced. I thought she was going to throw her chardonnay at me. But it was expensive chardonnay, so she decided to drink it instead.

Then Tina told me that she wasn't going to eat one bite because her mantra was "water during the day and wine at night."

"Oh, *that* sounds healthy..." Why did we go out to dinner? I wondered.

"I'll look like a pencil by the weekend," Tina informed me.

"You'll be dead by the weekend," I told her back.

I didn't want to eat alone, so we ended up looking for Alex's cookout after all. Alex seemed glad to see me; although, he was disappointed I had forgotten to bring wood. We cooked corn and steaks and then everyone left to go to his house to dance. Alex asked me about twelve times to come over. He even tried to hold my hand once. He ate dinner next to me and practically ignored everyone else. Lucinda was nowhere to be found.

I told him I'd come by. Maybe. But I veered off and drove directly home. I'd left all the lights on so I'd feel welcome, and Jackie was all excited to see me.

I was doing fine on my own, thank you very much. The files in my fabulous office had files in them. All my bills were paid. I had copies of all my bank statements. I had found the title to the house. Things were looking good. Who needed anyone, anyway? I was perfect, actually. Which was comforting. (I explained all this to Jackie.)

This was all very nice in theory, and I could certainly live by myself for the rest of my life and muddle through, but it would be nice to have some emotional, organizational, and monetary help, for God's sake! What was wrong with asking for a little assistance?

"Fine, Alex baby, in case you haven't noticed, I've taken care of the stupid roof and the insurance and just about everything else for the past seven months. Have I ever asked you to do anything? Noooo. I feel in control. The computers work, the oven and stove are new, I'm still selling houses, and I am in complete control of life. And, therefore, I don't need you. I never needed you. I loved you!"

Who was I talking to?

I'd programmed my cell phone, bought a Palm Pilot, and my computer obeyed me. The bills were paid; my credit report was okay, the kids seemed happy...

Timmy died. People did. He could be around, I thought. He may have fixed the transmission in my car, which had been making disturbingly funny noises, and the gas station guy told me it could cost up to a thousand dollars to fix. Then the noises simply stopped and the car ran beautifully.

"I bet that was Timmy; he loved playing with cars. I know he's around because I am feeling very happy," I said aloud, kind of dancing around to the Grateful Dead. What a name, I thought and stopped abruptly.

I decided to call the Knot and see if he had an opening the next morning. The Knot was the one person I didn't have to feel embarrassed about needing. If people didn't need him, he'd be out of business.

"I'm going to go crazy and end up like my brother." I decided to get right to the point.

He listened.

"Sometimes really sensitive people, or else really confused and needy people like Timmy, do become mentally unstable, but Timmy was wonderful. I'd be lucky to be like him."

"I am sure you share many of his qualities. That doesn't mean there aren't differences. You aren't him." Then he added, "You're doing really well. I'm proud of you."

"You're proud of *you*. Shrinks are so transparent." I was better, though. Sometimes. "You made me sad, angry, lonely, and scared."

"Carly, it was the only way for you to get better."

"I know I'm better, but I didn't want to get better. I wanted to get happy."

"And…now you can have both."

"I think I should sue you."

"For what, exactly?"

"I don't know. I guess I'd like to make you suffer a little."

He frowned.

"I promise, I'm kidding."

I felt that I might someday actually go through life without seeing him every week. But I don't know how anyone actually leaves his or her shrink for good. How does a person get that healthy?

"That floating feeling?" he asked.

"You know as well as I do that it's gone. There's nothing worse than a smug shrink. But you know what's really, really sad?"

"What's really, really sad?"

"I bet Timmy had that floating feeling when he died."

Dear Timmy:

How the hell could you leave me like that? You selfish, no-good creep!

Not nice. He's dead. Try again.

Dear Timmy:

Hope it was worth the swim race, babe. I think you would have liked my kids. I always think of you as watching them. I named

Jamie after you—Timothy James. I tried to call him Timmy but I would sob every time, so we ended up calling him Jamie.

You never met Paul. A good thing, too. You would have hated him. He was always critical. A little too anal for me.

Alex is fine, determined to act like my older brother, since, as you probably realize, I don't have a brother anymore.

Sometimes I think he is the love of my life, and always was, but it isn't working out so well. It's not your fault. And maybe you were completely right and he was just using me. I need to say, "I'm so sorry" to you, and I can't. You're not here, so I can't. But I really am, because you loved me and you wanted to protect me. So I hope you read this.

It's just that it's a hard time right now.

Normally I am absolutely fine, so I don't want you to be worried. This damn loser shrink wants me to write this ridiculous letter.

Drops were falling all over Jamie's lined paper, smudging the words.

I can't write anymore. I love you. Carly

Timmy died and Dad started wearing headphones. Alex ran away to California. Mom rarely went to a party again

I thought about all those dreams I'd had about him throughout the years—about the smile that wasn't quite happy, and the way he taught me to ski, the way he shielded me when Mom and Dad fought, and how empty and scared I felt when he went off to college, how little time we'd had, how I hated families where the kids didn't get along, because they had no clue what they had, how I idolized him so much more when he was no longer there, and the millions of times I'd forget and think, "Oh God, I have to tell Timmy that one," and then I'd realize, "Oh that's right, he's dead." I thought about how Alex was after Timmy died. I remembered the two of us down at the ocean jetty in East Hampton after everyone had headed back to the house.

The whole afternoon went downhill from there. I knew there was no one who could help—suddenly it seemed that absolutely no one in the entire world would be able to do that. It was one of those terrifying times you try to avoid when you know that no one can protect you, everyone leaves, everyone is separate, and if there's one really scary feeling to have, that is it.

Nothing was resolved. The eleven-year-old girl had taken over me again.

EIGHTEEN

The next morning I went over to Mom's house, since she was leaving for East Hampton for the entire summer, forcing my poor father to travel up there on weekends to see her. She's done this since they were married, so I decided it was none of my business.

Funny how everyone leaves at the exact same time.

Mom was upstairs packing and I lay curled up on her bed, like I always did as a child.

Mom looked down at her stomach and stuck it out. "Actually, I'm kind of fascinated by how horrible I look. Maybe this stomach could win a contest or something."

I ignored her, hoping this would work like it was supposed to with three-year-olds—don't reinforce childish behavior. "Well," she continued, "I'll look like a broomstick by September. I'm not going to darken the door of a grocery store the whole time I'm away. I'm not even going to cook an egg. I'm so tired of the whole bloody cooking process!"

"Great, Mom." I couldn't say much because she'd know (as mothers seem to) that I was a wreck.

"Anyway, thank God your father loves microwave dinners so much. I think he kind of enjoys it when I'm gone. He gets so much more done."

"Stop justifying it. You go up every year. He'll be fine."

I kept flipping through a magazine. She looked worried. Suddenly she blurted out, "I bet he goes into the hospital right before I leave and I'll be trapped here like a rat for weeks!"

"Go tomorrow morning, just in case," I told her. "You're packed, so what's stopping you? One day?"

Mom seemed thoughtful. Then she burst into this huge grin, as if I had told her I was engaged to a count.

"Brilliant! That's just brilliant! You're coming up soon, right?"

"For a few days, that's it."

"I'll try to think of someone to set you up with."

"I think it would be best if you let that one alone," I told her.

That afternoon I went for a late afternoon bike ride along the canal to clear out the cobwebs—going to East Hampton, the mixed feelings of Jamie and Kerry being gone, Alex and Lucinda together or not, John's betrayal (how long had he known?), and the fact that he never called again just when I was all freed up to have a fantastic romantic affair. Then I was talking to my Self about the merits of carrying a cell phone on the bike path just in case someone decided to strangle me (this was Washington, after all, not Kansas), when I heard, "What did you say?"

I was completely startled, and when I get startled I scream—kind of like you would if you thought you were about to be murdered. Then I looked up, and there was Alex. He was stopped on his bike and I had just gone right past him.

"For Christ's sake, you scared me to death!" I screeched.

"It's not like I snuck up on you and said boo." He seemed hurt. "We're on a bike path. It's three in the afternoon."

I felt myself going beet red. Then I remembered what I had looked like when I left the house—no make-up, hair wild and uncombed—something like a troll. I hoped he couldn't see me too clearly.

"At least it's foggy," I blurted out, totally flustered. Then, making things worse, I added, "It's better for biking I think. And fishing. Fish love fog."

He appeared to consider this. "I didn't know you were such an expert," he smiled. "It's nice to see you."

I felt awkward. I used to talk to Alex about everything. He's seen me in my nightgown. He's seen me with no make-up, bawling. But for some ridiculous reason, I suddenly didn't know how to respond to him.

He looked at me for a long moment. "I miss you. You know that." I had no idea what he meant. "It's confusing. You're confusing," he said. He was still watching me. I needed to leave, but I couldn't move my feet. Then he came up very close and put his hands on my arms. His face was by my face. I thought if he didn't kiss me, I'd have to hit him.

But he did. Finally.

I let him kiss me, that's all. I did one thing right, though, which was to follow my mother's advice: Always be the first to leave.

That night I decided to tackle my closet. I was going to ask Tina to help with the clothes issue (what to keep, what to toss), but then I thought about her orange hair and her white cowboy boots and reconsidered. She was rebellious. Hey, I wanted to be rebellious too. But then the kids would feel traumatized because they would think I was unstable and weird, and their lives were unstable and weird enough as it was.

I found a few odds and ends, such as all of my ski-racing awards from college. Most of them were just wooden plaques with an engraved silver medallion in the middle. But two or three of them were sterling silver cups so tarnished they were almost black. I used to have them on my dresser, all shiny and bright and proud. But Paul had told me it was tacky, so I hid them away.

I also found some really old pictures held together by a rubber band. There were a few of Timmy and me playing tennis in East Hampton. There was one of him holding me up over his head after I had won a tournament while I held the trophy up over mine. There were four or five of us sailing off Block Island with Alex. I remembered that we'd asked some lady on another boat to take a few pictures of the three of us. Timmy was at the wheel, holding up his glass of rum and Coke. Timmy was always holding something up when his picture was being taken. If it wasn't me, it was usually a drink or an award.

I even found my passport. I had hidden it in an old shoebox because I was scared it would get stolen, but then I forgot exactly where I'd hidden it. Not that I was going anywhere, but it was nice to know I could if I wanted to. I found the Victoria's Secret teddy I bought at least two years ago. I took it out of the bag and examined it. I put it on.

I needed a break from this closet business, so I went downstairs for some wine, came back up and lit a bunch of candles, put on some George Winston, put on make-up, and swirled around the room for a few minutes to try to feel like I existed in the present, not just the past. Then I heard someone calling me. The door opened and Alex was standing there.

"Why are you dressed like that?" he asked, walking right in without being invited.

"You didn't even knock! I could have been naked!"

He smiled. "My loss." He put his cheek near mine. "You're wearing perfume! Did you curl your hair?"

"Well, yes." I felt as if I'd just confessed to taking heroin.

"Are you okay? I called and called from downstairs but you didn't answer."

"Why do you always ask if I'm okay?"

He smiled. "It's my job." He looked around. In addition to the candles and the music, I had the bottle of wine in the ice bucket. "Are you expecting someone?"

"No. I started cleaning out my closet and I got kind of angry so I stopped."

"Interesting reaction." Then he smiled and said, "Damn! And here I thought you were waiting for me!" I knew he was joking, but I wasn't quite ready to play along. I was feeling vulnerable and I just didn't want Alex to see me that way.

"Well, you look awfully adorable."

What does that have to do with anything?

"Right! Sure thing! You can't just barge into *my* bedroom like you own the damn place and…"

"Okay. I'm sorry! Calm down. I'm sorry." He started to give me a hug but I pushed him away.

"I wouldn't sleep with you if you were the last person on earth." I looked around. I grabbed an old robe in the throw-away pile and covered myself. "You hate my house. I want you to leave."

"No I don't. God, Carly, you're wonderful!"

"You told me to improve."

"I know. I know that. Listen, I didn't mean it, first of all, and I should have called first. I just stopped by on the way home from work to see if you were okay."

"*Stop* asking if I'm okay. I'm perfectly okay." By this time I was a little teary because I was embarrassed and I didn't think the awards and the pictures and the teddy (with the tags still on) and the kids being gone helped. Alex was still holding me, but he was feeling my ribs.

"Are you becoming anorexic?" he asked.

"I've told you a thousand times that I'm fine!"

I couldn't breathe. I started heaving, and then I started sobbing. I have to stop having crying fits in front of men.

Alex noticed the pictures. "Oh, Carly, don't put yourself through this," he said.

We sat on the bed with the pictures. "You say the wrong things sometimes," I told him.

He just looked at me.

"I took all the price tags off my shoes." He had once told me it might be a good idea to do this after I bought them. I hadn't realized people noticed the bottom of your shoes.

He looked at me strangely. Like you do when you want someone, someone you've always wanted, and I felt that same hunger, unbearable, I just wanted him—his shoulders, his smell, his arms, so different from John, where it was just sex—this was a wanting. We were so close. I almost couldn't stand it.

"He always has loved me," I thought. I was sure. Our eyelashes were practically touching. We both were breathing hard. His lips were so close that I was trembling from wanting him for so long, thinking about this for so long, and being this close to him. Never had we been this close, allowed ourselves to be, except the night Timmy died. I reached to touch his arm but instead jammed it into the night table, knocking the little velvet box with John's earrings and note onto the floor. I watched in horror as Alex bent down. He held one of the earrings up to the light. He glanced at the note. The only time I have ever put anything back where it belonged, I remember thinking.

By the time my arm got to his, he shoved it away and stood up. "Hey, give my best to John. Sorry I barged in." And just as he reached the door he turned and said, "Okay?" only it was in a mean, cold, sarcastic tone. There was nothing to say;

he'd made up his mind. I turned over on my stomach to avert his eyes.

"Asshole." I muttered.

"Excuse me?"

I scrambled off the bed.

"You're as pathetic as you were when you jumped back like I was a poisonous snake the night Timmy died and, gee, Alex, maybe you just like to tease me, get me all hot and bothered, see if I still like you or something that cruel and demented. Well, did you get your kicks, Mr. Flirt? Are you okay, asshole?"

"Gee, Carly," he replied in my exact voice, which made me even madder, "when did you turn into a slut? Want to be fucking two boys at the same time? John not enough for you? Want one if the other isn't around? Nice game to play."

"*You* came over here." I wanted to kill him. " Remember? This is all your fault. And like you weren't fucking Lolita."

"Lucy is none of your business."

"And John is none of yours!"

This expression I knew I'd never forget crossed his face— defeat, pain, sadness, loss, but it was really quick, and of course I would have told him I wasn't even *with* John, and that I loved *him* more than anything, but I was way too mad and he had, after all, seduced me and then called me a slut.

"Fuck you, Alex. You don't even know what the hell you're talking about."

"Fuck you too, Carly. But I'm sure you're doing plenty of that."

He turned and slammed the door and I ran and threw it open, screaming as he ran down the stairs, "I am not a slut! How dare you call me a slut!"? At the top of my voice, long after he had gone.

Jackie and I left Washington that day, spur of the moment, vaguely in the direction of East Hampton, but in no hurry to get there. We stopped at the Jersey Shore for a night and spent two nights in New York so Jackie could see all the tall buildings and get a feel for a real city. A city with some real men, I thought, pounding the pavement and talking to myself every time I thought about Alex. I tried to forget. I thought if a person could be somewhere to forget something, New York would be where you could find whatever it was you lost and replace it. New York had everything.

I spoiled Jackie with tons of toys and met some adorable men while walking around with gorgeous Jackie. We were going to spend the afternoon at Central Park, but since Jackie, not used to other dogs, and convinced she was a German shepherd, attacked all the other dogs, I had to scoop her up and run out of there. We stayed in a hotel on the West Side, which wasn't too expensive; at least it was cheaper than my parking bill. We ordered room service and watched all sorts of movies. The next morning we left for East Hampton while I still had enough money for tolls.

I was getting more irritated, confused, hurt, and almost furious that Alex, although it was my fault for not forcing him to listen to the truth. I didn't even try to tell him what had happened with John. Maybe a part of me didn't want to. Maybe it was pride. Alex had never assured me that it was over with Lucinda/nymph.

The thought with Alex and Lucy together made me feel sick. I drove way too fast and angrily all the way to East Hampton and Mom wasn't even home. I dropped off Jackie and my luggage at home before heading to the beach for a swim. I'd called Mom all morning from the highway (highly illegal, but so was speeding) but there was no answer. I showered at our beach cabana, my favorite place to be—a mini cottage right on the water—then walked up to the clubhouse and golf course to see if anything interesting was going on. There was an ambulance and about a hundred people. It looked like that many, at least. I made my way through since I knew every single person at the club—and there on the stretcher was my mother.

If Mom was suffering from a heart attack, I knew instinctively I would make it worse since she had no idea I was coming up, but she didn't see me because her whole face was filled with blood.

"Carly, Carly, your mother!!!" All these people were grabbing me trying to tell me what happened…"She got hit straight in the eye with a golf ball! Your mother lost her eye! It's somewhere on the damn course! Look at her head, she could be dead from shock!"

Voices I couldn't recognize were screaming at me as I pushed my way past them to the paramedics. "I'm her daughter, get me to her." My heart was pounding out of control, there was blood everywhere, and Mom did, truly, look very dead. I climbed into the ambulance as they were lifting her in and took her hand.

"Mommy? It's your daughter. Remember me?" I asked softly.

"You can ride with her, I guess," a paramedic told me grudgingly.

"Let them try to kick me out," I thought.

"Of course I remember you. Do you think I've lost my mind?" Mom's voice bellowed back. "The question is what are you doing here? Trying to scare me half to death? I'm thrilled, of course, but a little warning to a woman over seventy is the polite thing to do. Let's say I was having an affair?"

"I...I called from the expressway a thousand times." I was feeling foolish.

"Anyway, dear girl," she squeezed my hand as more blood squirted out from the gauze that was covering her face, making her look exactly like the exorcist, "I simply got hit straight in the eyeball from about one foot away, and of course I am thrilled beyond words that you're here. I love you so much." I couldn't tell if she was crying, of course. "I thought my eye had come out. I bent down and looked everywhere for it but I couldn't see a damn thing from all the blood. Then some doctor ordered me not to move and everyone held me straight up, all the blood near my brain, you see."

"No talking," Paramedic Two told us with authority. And every time Mom started to, she was forced to shut up. They were trying to stop the blood from swelling her brain, they explained. They were trying to save her eye.

"I'll be out in an hour of so," she whispered to me as the ambulance pulled into Southampton Hospital. "We'll sneak out to a few parties after that."

It would be a long week, taking care of Mom.

Thank God they kept her in the hospital for two days because I couldn't have handled her. She'd been home for less than an hour when I tried to put her in the car and drive her back to the hospital. Mom was worse than a naughty, spoiled seven-year-old. Her instructions were to lay perfectly still and not even moving her head one inch due to the possibility of a brain swell, which could be fatal, and damage to her eye. The doctors and specialists were very clear about this. The dressings needed to be changed twice a day. She could sit up on a slant while eating. Never lean head below heart. Bedpan instead of bathroom. The rules were clear.

The first morning she was home, Mom woke up at six and made coffee and our breakfast...eggs, bacon, hot cereal, pancakes, the works. I just could not beat her.

"Mom, come on, you need to stay in bed." I was exhausted. The kitchen was bustling.

"I can't stay in bed all day."

"It's six-thirty in the morning!"

"Coffee makes me a little hyper; perhaps I should go for a walk."

"I swear I'll commit you if you don't get better."

"I am doing much better. I can see very well, actually." She seemed a little hurt. "The doctor's going to let me go see the ocean today," she announced. "I can feel it in my bones."

She insisted on drawing and taking her own bath, one of the worst things to do, because you had to bend your head down to do it. She claimed she could do it with her head perfectly upright and very still.

I also caught her in the pool. She was just standing there looking like a cross between Stevie Wonder, with her head bobbing from side to side, and Jackie O, with her huge sunglasses that took up her entire face as well as the sides of her head. All you could see was her smile.

She was singing, "Someone left the cake out in the rain, I don't think that I can take it, cause it took so long to bake it, and I'll never have that recipe again, Oh no..."

She stopped.

"God, I loved Stratton. That Lewis, now there was a piano player."

I vaguely remembered him, playing songs as Mom sang. Mom loved après-ski. "The only thing better than skiing is taking your boots off at the end of the day," she once told me. I was eleven years old at the time.

"Mom, I think the doctors were very clear about your pool theory."

"Really, what did they say again?"

"'Absolutely not.' I'm pretty sure you remember."

"Well, for Christ's sake, don't you dare tell them."

We had to go to the hospital every day. The doctors told me that she absolutely could not get jolted in the car or it would cause a second bleed, which could be very dangerous. That left me the responsibility of keeping every single tourist away from our car, every person in the middle of summer who happened to be racing down the overcrowded highway from East Hampton to Southampton, where the hospital was located. The doctors advised us that Mom should be back in the hospital, where she couldn't move, and when they asked me if she was being perfectly still in every single way at home, I felt as if they were looking into the depths of my soul.

Mom rambled on in the car about how today would be the day she'd be given the green light, and how we would be playing golf in a day or two, although she would have a perfect excuse for losing to me.

The twelfth was supposed to be "make or break" day at the hospital. We went into the all-too-familiar office. Mother had a different doctor every four days. I always hated this one. He didn't understand her.

He asked her to read the eye chart.

"It's a four," she told him proudly. She thought she had memorized it, which was how she got a driver's license.

"No, it's an eight. Next?"

"That is a definite B."

"Actually, that is a twelve."

"Oh."

"You are going to the hospital for two weeks or you will lose your eyesight." His voice was gritty.

"I can't!" she protested. "It's my time with my daughter."

"Mom, we can do tons of things in Washington. I'll see you every day!"

She ignored me. "It's summer. Couldn't I come in September? I'll be very still until then."

She could tell he was going to say no, so she raised her hand. "I'm seventy years old," she announced. "It's my decision."

So I got her out of there, blind as a bat. We had lunch by the bay, took a walk across the golf course, had whiskey sours by the pool, and went to the Palm for dinner. She couldn't see a thing, but she seemed extremely happy anyway.

NINETEEN

A few days later, Mom announced she was returning to Washington long enough to have an eye operation in Baltimore, since they were "the best in the country and the doctors up here are idiots."

The next day, the day she was leaving, Mom wanted to go down to the beach. East Hampton has some of the most beautiful, clean, open beaches on earth, and although the town is overrun with visitors, the beaches are still un-crowded. I never could understand the point of coming to East Hampton if you didn't love the beach.

We sat down close to the edge. Mom looked wistfully at the surf.

"That ocean's just gorgeous today, like whipped cream, you know? I mean, I would go in there right this second if it weren't for that damn undertow. I think I could almost go in, I just don't think I could get out."

"Getting out is key," I said.

"Well, yes. I suppose the lifeguard could pull me out, but that gets embarrassing."

"Three times a summer should be your limit, or at least do it on weekdays. Fewer people watching," I pointed out.

"It's not that bad, I don't turn blue or anything!" she retorted, slightly defensive. We were silent for a while, watching the surf. Suddenly Mom picked up the glass of wine she had brought to the beach and pointed to a seagull. "Cheers to you, Timbo," she toasted.

"Mom!" I was mortified.

"Oh, who knows, I think he takes on different forms and comes for little visits."

I didn't say anything.

"Listen, if it helps me, what difference does it make?"

That made sense, so I toasted the seagull too. "I can see the resemblance. They have the same eyes," I told her. And she laughed more than I had heard her in a long time.

"Are you sure you want to stay up here alone, doll?"

"Just for a few days." I had made the decision to stay earlier that day.

"Well," she sounded slightly pouty, "I could get a complex you know, since I have to practically beg you to visit me, and then, when I have to go home, you want to be here."

"Oh, God, Mom, if you had behaved you wouldn't have to go anywhere."

"Well, we had some fun, didn't we? Fooling those doctors…but I wish we could have played more!"

"Everything was great. You were an excellent patient," I told her.

"Next time I come, you have to swear on your life you'll come up so we can go swimming. I could almost go right now, but..."

"Next time. I promise."

After I took her to the airport, I returned to the house and tried not to feel empty without her there. At thirty-six, I would call that semi-pathetic. I knew someone in school nicknamed Path. It was short for pathetic, but I don't think he knew that. At least I hope he didn't.

I decided to go back to the beach. As I tried to figure out why I wanted to stay, I decided the beach was probably the reason. I was going to ride my bike, but it had clouded up and looked like rain, so I decided to walk. I put on Timmy's hotshot sailor jacket that we could never throw away, but it felt so big and fancy that I felt a little foolish in it, so I ended up wearing my father's beat-up raincoat instead. The whole thing was ironic, because Timmy had been a slob and Dad had always been immaculate, but you couldn't tell from their jackets.

It was only a mile or so to the beach. I walked down to where I had been with Mom earlier, and then continued to the jetty where Timmy had learned to surf while I sat in the sand

and watched. If I were trying to cheer myself up, this was definitely not the way to do it.

You had to be cool to hang out in that spot when we were kids. First of all, you had to be brave enough to ride the waves in any surf and not worry about crashing into the rocks. This was a local beach—"Georgica Beach" or "Coast Guard Beach"—and they were impatient with tourists who didn't understand the ocean because, for one reason, down by the three jetties there were no lifeguards. I think they made an exception for us because Timmy was such a great surfer and I was his sister.

Timmy loved it at that the first jetty more than any place else in the world. Everyone got high, there was always plenty of beer, Timmy was a natural surfer, the girls wore no tops (except for me and a few others), and he was away from Mom and Dad. What a relief that was! We weren't under their thumb for once in our lives. Timmy could still surf with the best and then go back home and put on whites and win the sixteen-and-under tennis finals.

I sat down on the jetty at the very place we threw Timmy's ashes into the sea. That year, Dad had dragged Mom to California for three weeks in August, so Timmy and I had the house to ourselves for almost the whole month. We were ecstatic. Alex came up and joined us. They were both twenty-one and it was right before they were going back for their senior year at the

University of Vermont. I wanted to go with them, of course. In fact, I wanted to do everything with them, and I pretty much got my wish that one summer.

We loved being away from Mom and Dad so that we could try drugs and healthy things like that. We discovered Long Island iced teas, which had about every kind of liquor imaginable in them, and we thought this was hilarious since we were on Long Island and we had never even heard of Long Island iced teas before. Luckily, we balanced all those late nights with long hikes and discussions about philosophy, although these discussions usually took place around three in the morning so we rarely remembered them the next day. At the time, of course, we thought we were brilliant. At least that's what we told Mom and Dad.

I had graduated from National Cathedral that May (finally), but I hadn't been able to fully commit to a college. Of course I wanted to go to the University of Vermont and follow Alex and Timmy, but that seemed awfully unimaginative and needy. Obviously, I firmly believed that Alex and I were soul mates, so why couldn't I just get it over with so Alex could marry me as I had planned since I was eleven and Timmy would be our best friend?

Because it would show no independence, imagination, knowledge, and respect for myself, and it would display cowardliness on my part. These were the reasons teachers, counselors, and just about everyone else kept telling me my entire senior year.

For some reason, I had stubbornly stood my ground and was given until the end of the summer to make my final decision.

Alex, Timmy, and I did a thousand things that unforgettable August, some disturbing and some simply heavenly. I remember being worried about Timmy when we borrowed a friend's boat and went to Block Island for a few days. Timmy always insisted on taking the helm. His restless spirit never allowed him to just sit still and watch the changing sky and the birds and the waves splashing on the bow.

I was furious with him on that trip. In fact, I left on the third morning, at around 6:30 a.m. The color of the sky was purplish pink. Timmy was on the deck, listening to Fleetwood Mac, trying to wake Alex so he could tell him about his master plan to take the boat to Martha's Vineyard "right now."

That sounds normal, Timmy! I thought. It's so innocent, a little extra sailing trip. Does it have anything to do with the fact that you haven't gone to sleep yet? That this is the third night you've been up all night? That I've found three or four rolled-up dollar bills left haphazardly around the cabin along with a few crumpled-up pieces of plastic licked clean? How stupid do you think I am, anyway?

Block Island was Timmy's kind of town—so many bars, so many people. People who hated sleep as much as he did, who watched the sun rise with sweaty hands and beating hearts. People who lined up for bathrooms day and night, inhaling white powder on the lids of dirty toilet seats. Alex never did drugs, but Timmy always found someone to do them with, usually a girl.

He could have it. I decided to fly home. They could take the boat back.

They arrived back in East Hampton the very next day. I was surprised to see them. Timmy looked half dead. His slanted brown eyes were sunken into his skull. When I checked on him after he had been asleep for eighteen hours, he was curled up in exactly the same position he used to sleep in when he was around twelve years old.

Three days later he was back to normal and we swam in the surf with some of his friends. As we were walking home, he swore he'd never touch drugs again. And then he hugged me as hard as anyone could, for a long, long time.

"How come you're always taking care of me?" he asked.

"Because if anything happened to you, I'd be stuck with Mom and Dad," I told him.

"I'm still allowed to drink, right?"

"Timmy, I'm not your mother! I just don't want you dead!"

We kept walking. "I don't want to be dead, either!" He was kind of prancing around, half wet and wearing only his bathing suit. "There are too many girls in the world."

"You seem to have just about all of them."

Then he stopped walking and half whispered, "Guess what that cute guy we met on the beach said about you today?"

"What? Tell me right now!"

"You like him, I can tell!" That wasn't necessarily true. I just thought he was cute.

"Tell me what he said! Right this second!"

"He's rich too. And smart. And nice! You'd make a great couple." He was always teasing me, but not the kind that hurt.

"Stop it! I want to know!"

He stopped walking. "He said, 'She may have the best legs on the beach, but what really got to me are her bedroom eyes.'"

I couldn't tell if he were kidding or not. I studied him. "Liar," I said.

"I told him if he went near you, I'd have to kill him."

"I'll be an old maid if I stick around you."

That night we all went out to Savannah's for steak dinners and then to the Wild Rose dancing. Timmy was wonderful the whole time, and I danced with Alex and the boy from the beach to almost every song. We spent the next week with whoever wanted to join us doing whatever we wanted. We took a bike ride to Montauk and had lobster, coleslaw, and french fries overlooking the boats. We went water-skiing around Gardiner's Island, rode down the beach in Alex's jeep, and sailed to Block Island for the night. Everything floated.

The last night we were there, the three of us made dinner for all the friends we had known since we were kids. There were at least twenty of us at two picnic tables in the backyard, with the sunset behind us, and the temperature going from hot to chilly, the way it does in August. It was a night no one wanted to end. Timmy never wanted nights to end. He was always the last one to bed. But we all felt it that night.

After dinner, everyone piled into two jeeps. We brought wood and coolers of wine and beer and headed to the beach. We built a fire in the sand and drank and made toasts to the end of the summer, and some people were dancing. The ocean was as serene that night as I had ever seen it. You could almost make out the red buoys that were anchored way out to sea. We never really knew what their purpose was, although they had always been there. Timmy and Alex had swum to them a few times, but not very often, because they were really pretty far.

Alex and I danced a little bit, and I danced with the boy who liked my eyes as well. Then someone suggested swimming and everyone decided that was a grand idea. Some people stripped off all their clothes, others kept on their underwear. I was one of those. Alex was, too. There weren't any waves to ride, so we were just sort of bobbing around in different directions, and Alex was beside me. That's when he started to kiss me. I had waited so long for it that I almost cried out.

Thank God I had some practice in sexual encounters, but not with anyone like Alex. I tried not to think about it. He had to kind of hold me above the water because I could barely touch and since he's six-one he had no problem. We had just begun tentative touching, which was the most exciting thing that had happened to me in my entire eighteen years, because it was with Alex. He was moving very slowly, which I absolutely loved, except I was impatient sometimes. I was just about to become more aggressive because I'd had all these feelings pent up since I was very young and now I could express them all in the dark in the water where nothing felt real enough to be ashamed about.

His hands were going all over me and thank God water made a person feel thin and smooth and light. Also, in water there's no awkward shifting of positions and negotiations regarding clothes. All the awkward necking rituals were pleasantly missing. Of course it would be perfect. I was with Alex. How else could it possibly be?

"Hey, Alex, is that my sister?" Timmy glided underwater and popped up about five feet away from us. He could have whispered, but no, he said it so loudly it carried on the sea.

Alex let me go so fast I felt as if I'd been sprung off a diving board. The three of us were still. I tried to cover myself up. "Oh, fuck you, Timmy," I finally said in a low, slow tone. At that age, I thought you only had one chance in life, and if you didn't take it you'd never have the chance again. I didn't yet realize that (for some people) life is relatively long. I turned and swam back to shore without stopping. I dried off and put on my clothes and walked the mile back to the house. Nothing would be the same again; I knew it for sure.

I was furious with Timmy because I knew he'd come up to us in order to protect his little sister, and I wanted him to stop thinking of me that way. Eighteen was ancient. Mother was married at that age! How dare he ruin my life? Alex would never approach me again, I was sure, and all because of my nosy, controlling older brother.

I sat on the porch for a while, stewing and waiting for everyone to come back. No one came. I wondered if I should walk back to the beach. But I remembered I had a car. So I drove back and walked down to the fire. Someone must have built it up again because the flames were shooting into the dark. No one was ready for the party to be over any time soon. The music was still blaring Van Morrison, "And I want to make love to you tonight I can't wait 'til the morning has come…"

I walked up to them, planning to be extremely aloof, but Alex and Timmy were nowhere to be seen. Someone was passing a pipe. Some people were still dancing. Most were around the fire, talking and gesturing and laughing. The group had grown. That's what happens at beach parties in East Hampton: friends tell friends and pretty soon they're huge.

"Do you guys know where Alex and Timmy are?" I asked the group, kind of embarrassed. Then I had to ask again, because no one was paying attention. Finally someone answered.

"They raced across to the buoys. But that was a while ago." And then there was a murmuring of voices, "Did you guys see them? No…that was at least an hour ago…I thought I heard them talking…no, they had a fight, right? Then it turned into a bet…who could get there and back fastest…well, they should have been back by now…"

"So no one saw them?" I persisted.

And there was murmuring again from many voices around the fire. "No, we were kind of waiting…is there any more wine? They should be back, right? It's really late…but it's a really far way to go. That was so stupid of them, ya know? Oh, they were just drunk…" And then there was only silence. Timmy and Alex were out there, and it was two in the morning, and they weren't back. It had been well over an hour since I left them. There was a boat with a motor, hidden in the dunes, that we used on occasion, and everyone by the fire, people Timmy and I had known our whole lives, seemed frozen in the sand.

Then everyone was moving. Someone ran up to a house to call Fire and Rescue or whomever he could, and two guys who had played golf with Timmy and Alex that day started toward the boat. I ran after them and we dragged it down the beach to the water, started the engine, and went off. Then we turned around while someone else ran over to give us a flashlight. It all seemed to be taking place in slow motion, as if I were an observer, or participating in a dream.

Unfortunately, there was only a quarter moon, but it did its best to shine on us. So did the millions of stars.

As we approached the buoy, we spotted someone flailing around in the water. We called to him but couldn't hear anything over the noise of the motor as we sped toward him.

It was Alex; half incoherent, blabbering away so much we could barely get him into the boat. "You have him, right? Where the hell did he go? He was right next to me! I was swimming as fast as I could. He turned around, didn't he? Left me alone in the fucking ocean! Goddamn joker! I told him not to go! And that stubborn jerk goes anyway! Here I'm swimming as fast as I can to follow him and he goes and turns around on me! I was scared to death!"

"Alex, shut up for a sec! You can barely breathe!" I ordered.

But he wasn't listening. "Where is he, damn it? I've called and called for him! Tell him he scared me to death! Where the hell is he?"

We'd forgotten to bring towels, but there were some old smelly ones in one of the compartments and I tried to wrap him up in them. "Where is he, damn it! I've been calling for hours!"

"He's not with us," I finally said. "He didn't come back. He was with you."

The ocean was still and quiet. We could see the campfire in the distance; we could even see bodies moving about. But we saw no movement on the water. One of the boys called in an emergency on the radio. We drove around with our flashlight. I started to laugh. "This is a dream, right? Or a prank! You guys, it's not funny! This is Timmy we're talking about! The best swimmer in the whole damn world!"

"He drank enough for ten people tonight," said the name-less driver, almost under his breath.

I was going after him when the other guy, holding the flashlight, screamed, "Wait!"

They had spotted him. He was face down and stiller than Timmy was capable of being. We pulled up to him, Alex and someone else jumped in the water, and we dragged him onto the boat. I was screaming at him, hitting him, punching him, hugging him, but I was, of course, doing nothing useful, so the others had to hold me back while Alex did CPR and the flashing boat from the East Hampton Fire Department got noisier as it approached us, stirring up the still water. But in the end, no one could do anything, because he was already dead.

TWENTY

The clouds had passed, but the sun was low on the water, and I figured I had left Mom at least four hours ago, and although it was still July, I realized it must be late. I didn't want to leave until I could forgive. Who should I forgive? Myself, for being a childish brat? Maybe Timmy, for his carelessness, his disregard for the rules of nature, or for the fact that he felt compelled to over-protect me, but it felt unfair to blame someone who had died, who had such a love/hate relationship with life that the only way to survive was to challenge it.

Or, I could forgive Alex because the bet was so foolish, or even the ocean for taking my only brother, whom I adored before I learned that no one is to be idolized.

I sat on the jetty, searching the surf for an answer. I thought of praying, although I was angry enough with God at the moment that I wasn't sure I could. Nevertheless, I decided to give it a try. So I stayed very still. Then I called out in a strong voice, "Timbo, God, whoever, I need to get over this. You know? It's really screwing up my life. And I'm feeling really, really lonely!"

I sobbed and sobbed until the sun was at the horizon.

It made me feel much better, eventually. And then this really weird thing happened. I realized that Timmy was gone, but I had Jamie and Kerry, and suddenly I knew that no one had to protect me anymore. I just needed to protect my kids. I wasn't eighteen, and I didn't need Paul, or Alex, or anyone. Alex could go to hell, for all it mattered. He could stop his worried looks, protective hugs, and asking "Are you okay?" He knew part of me was stuck at eighteen. The Knot was right, I had stayed there, feeling left behind. And then I realized that it didn't matter who else left me, because I wasn't that young girl anymore. I could comfort her as if she were someone else, because she wasn't me.

I walked back home feeling lighter. My parents' house felt to me as if it were on a remote island in Nova Scotia. The floors creaked when I walked on them, but the sound didn't bother me at all, and it had petrified me when I was a kid. The house was a great mix of old and new. It had a wonderful cozy feeling with large, overstuffed chairs in the living room and thousands of books on the bookshelves. The kitchen had a fantastic gas stove, a circular oak table, a fireplace, and floor-to-ceiling windows looking out on the back porch and lawn.

That's as far as I got. I turned on the stereo, put my hair up, and poured a glass of wine. Then I went out to the porch and curled up in my very favorite wicker rocking chair to finish a wizard book the Knot had ordered me to read. I liked it because people didn't really die, they just changed forms. Plus the book was short, with big writing. I decided I'd reward myself and read something decadent when I finished it. I could read any book I wanted.

According to Deepak Chopra, another person who was famous now, anyone could be a wizard. And wizards knew everything and loved everyone. All of us could have *every single thing we wanted* just by asking the universe for it! So I was pretty excited about the whole concept.

I was going to call Tina with the good news, except, unfortunately, there was one catch; you had to follow a few simple rules to live this life of bliss. Rule Number One: You couldn't fall in love. Ever. You had to love everyone with all your heart, you couldn't play any emotional games, and you had to love your enemies just as much as your friends, and you couldn't judge anyone.

I didn't think Tina (or I) could adhere to Rule Number One. It wasn't fair, because men had a much better chance of becoming wizards. Which means they'd all get everything they wanted—money, houses in Aspen, and trips. Because men didn't usually like to fall in love, it wasn't that important to them anyway, whereas it was very important for most women to be involved somehow with some man. That's why we had a tendency to make the tremendous mistake of staying in relationships that were absolutely horrible for us. We thought it was better than nothing. (However, I decided I was doing quite well at breaking this habit. I would give myself a B.)

Fast cars, football, cigars, and power meant more to men than romantic relationships. So men were once again the lucky ones. They were not the housewives, and they could be the wizards.

However, men might have a hard time with the next rule: Wizards didn't care if they had any possessions or not. They could have everything if they wanted to (just by asking the universe), but they didn't *need* anything. They had their souls, and apparently that is all anyone needs to be happy.

I thought about this. I liked having my house. I thought a little money in the bank was a good thing. I liked my car and the new navigation system in it. So I'd failed Rule Number Two. But men *loved* big houses and fancy cars and making as much money as possible. It could even sometimes seem (although I was sure it simply was not true) that they loved these things more than they loved people. If they had to choose a relationship over, say, a prestigious house near a golf course, well, I think we all know what the outcome would be: "Where are my clubs?" So they were going to have a huge disadvantage on that one. And you couldn't fake it, because it was the connection to the cosmos, and the cosmos knew everything.

I felt a little bad about thinking that Tina would never be a wizard when she'd been such a great friend for so long. I left the porch and went inside to call her.

"Did you get sick of taking care of me? Because I love you and I am really grateful you did."

"Where are you?" she demanded.

"I'm in East Hampton."

"Are you having an affair or something?"

"No. I'm here by myself."

"I dyed my hair brown. I look like a ferret." She paused. "God, I haven't seen you in ages!"

"I was thinking we should go on a trip."

"You *are* on a trip."

"I mean, like, to Paris or something. Just us girls."

That certainly cheered her up. When I was living with Paul, I could never go anywhere with her because he disapproved. And all last year, I was too overwhelmed and broke to go anywhere. Well, that was all over now. I'd get someone to take care of the kids, and off we'd go because we were adventurous, independent women. And I could afford it because while I was taking care of my stubborn mother, my manager had agreed to cover for me, and one of my clients had bought a huge, expensive house.

"I'm number one in the office now," I told Tina.

"That's pretty good, since you've been there maybe once all year."

"Not true! I was there so much, the receptionist complained. She thinks I have a temper."

"You do have a temper."

"Paris in April," I said. And we hung up.

I decided to make some eggs for dinner. Another great thing about being single was you could eat weird things whenever you wanted. Then maybe I'd walk into town, like Mom and Timmy and I used to do when Dad was in Washington working and could only come on weekends. Walking into town was one of my favorite things because it meant Timmy and Mom had no plans that night, and they would be with me. Mom let us get chocolate from White's Pharmacy. I always chose white chocolate because I thought the pharmacy was named after it. Later, when I found out that wasn't true, I diversified a little.

Sometimes we went to movies at the Old Post Office Theater before East Hampton built a theater as big as an airport. I remember seeing "Lord of the Flies." Timmy got so upset, we had to leave. We'd go to the duck pond with stale bread to feed the ducks and run around the trails. Timmy and I always went to this particular statue on a hidden trail because it was so scary. We would leave the statue a nickel, just to play it safe. It was a very foreboding statue at the time, but when I found it again this year it was only two feet tall. It looked like a gray, abandoned china doll.

When we went to the beach, Mom insisted on teaching us everything about the ocean before we could go in. We knew how to lie flat on the ocean bottom if a big wave was going to crash right before us, how to ride the waves without breaking our necks, and how to dive through them without being tossed backwards.

"You respect the ocean. Never forget," she told us constantly.

Sometimes Mom fed us hot roast beef sandwiches on soft French bread in the evening, and Timmy and I would play tag with the neighbors on their sprawling lawn.

I always felt a little guilty dreading Fridays when Dad would come up. We'd pick him up at the airport and tell him about our week, and by then Mom had already transformed herself. She looked like a queen. When we got home, Dad shaved and showered and changed into a tux. They'd go to two or three parties, and on the weekends Timmy usually went out with friends as well, so I was there alone.

Cooking my eggs, I suddenly felt guilty again about dreading my father's arrival. I never really appreciated that my unusual opportunities—skiing or going to East Hampton—were possible only because of him. I decided to call him.

"Hello?"

"Mom, it's Carly. Is Dad there?"

"Aren't you even going to ask me about my eye? That dreadful doctor told me I would have to have two operations! I marched right out of there."

"Mom, he's one of the best eye surgeons in the world."

"Are you alright?" She was suddenly worried.

"I'm fine. Promise. I just want to talk to Dad."

"Do you need money or something?"

This was irritating, since I never asked them for money. "No, I just want to talk to him." Finally I could hear her in the background yelling, "T.J. (Timothy James), it's your daughter." Then, back to me, "Oh, Christ, he's got those things on his head." The phone slammed down. "T.J., take off those damn earphones and get on the phone! It's your daughter!"

He picked up the phone. "Hello? Dear? Are you alright?"

"Hi, Dad. I'm fine."

"What can I do?" Pause. "Is it money or something?"

"Dad, have I ever asked you for money? I just wanted to know if you wanted to have lunch next week."

"Really?" He sounded quite pleased.

"What's going on?" It was Mom; she had picked up the other phone.

"Mom!" I was exasperated. "I just want to talk to Dad for a sec. I'll call you tomorrow. Promise." She hung up, a little harder than necessary. "How's Wednesday?"

"Just the two of us?" he asked.

"Yup."

"Is there a particular reason?"

"I miss you. Is a daughter allowed to miss her father?"

He laughed. He seemed surprised and happy about it, and we hung up.

My timing was terrible because now my eggs were cold and I could never eat them cold, which is why I always eat eggs really fast. I didn't really want them in the first place. I went upstairs to take a bath. I loved the tubs in that house because they were the deep, old-fashioned kind.

That was another good thing about being single: I could put on my raggedy red robe and no one would say a thing. I could dance in the living room naked if I wanted to. (Well, I did have kids, so that would only work if they were away.) AND I could steal all the covers. I didn't need any man unless he liked me just the way I was.

So I was a little disorganized. He'd have to accept it. Alex would never think of me as an adult. There was too much history. I was just going to forget about him. I planned to try to be his friend when I got back, but never as close as we had been. Instead, I'd concentrate on me—I'd improve my French, go to Paris, take a dance class, make the kids hot roast beef sandwiches, and walk them to town.

I did like Alex's hands, though. And I liked the way he laughed. I liked the way he danced to "Fly Me to the Moon" and held me close. I liked the way he played soccer with Jamie and always put Kerry on his back. Well, I could do those things without him.

And, yes, I loved Alex's big shoulders, and the fact that he was a doctor didn't hurt. But I didn't need him to take care of me. I'd keep my nail appointments and go to the Knot and work harder and make sure the kids ate nutritious dinners every night.

I was glad I didn't go to town. I might have run into some of my childhood friends who I hadn't seen in years and it would remind me too much of Timmy, and I had done enough reminiscing for one day.

TWENTY-ONE

I had just gotten out of the tub, thrown on a shirt and jeans and had my hair upside down to dry when the phone rang. Being addicted to caller I.D., I panicked. Mom and Dad didn't have caller I.D. in East Hampton. Anyone could be calling. Even Paul. Or my mother. Or it could be a stranger wanting to know if anyone were there whom he could come over and murder. The phone just kept ringing because my parents also didn't own an answering machine, which was also annoying. Finally, I picked it up and it was Alex.

"Look outside," he said.

At least they had a cordless phone. I pulled up the shade just enough to see out the window, and there he was on the street, standing by his car.

"Come on, let's go," he called up to me, as if I were expecting him. "Alex!" I practically jumped up and down. And then I stopped, staring at myself in the long, silver-framed mirror in my bedroom, watching my eyes and face change to a child's, *"Pick me, love me, don't leave me, I'll do anything..."*

"Oh, Carly, you're not ten years old. You don't have to accept just anyone. You have a choice," I told the mirror.

"No, I have to have him, no matter what."

"Never wear 'I have settled' on your forehead again. Never beg for someone's love." The reflection stared back.

"Oh, the hell with you," I scolded the mirror.

I grabbed my purse and went downstairs to the car.

"Don't say a word. Just get in," Alex told me. So I did.

He put the top down, put on a U2 song; *You say that in love there are no rules. Baby, you're so cruel."* It seemed he didn't want me to talk. We drove to the beach. It took less than three minutes. We walked down to the ocean and he peeled off his clothes and dove in. I thought he was testing me, to see how daring I was, how adventurous. Personally, I hate when men do that. It just proves they don't know what they want. They want a feminine, sexy, subservient, quiet woman *and* an adventurous, daring, athletic, beautiful, multitalented, smart-but-not-too-smart woman who will jump into the pitch-black ocean stark naked at the drop of a hat. Someone who will listen to them, but have her own opinions, and who will tell them she loves them, but never let them know for sure. I'd played this game with Alex long ago, before I even met Paul. I went in the ocean that time and practically lost my virginity and it killed my brother. But was I his girlfriend the next day? Or a friend, even? No. He took off. He just left, right after we scattered Timmy's ashes and I gave the finger to the clueless waves. He didn't even go to the memorial service at National Cathedral in Washington.

So what did I do the night I went swimming with Alex? I got furious with my own brother for meddling when, most likely, Alex had never liked me at all and was just trying to do the typical male thing and get in my pants (although they were off at the time since we were just in our underwear, so he had it pretty easy from the start), and Timmy probably knew that and had every reason to try to protect me. And now I could never tell him he was right and I was wrong because he was dead. And maybe Alex was just the same as then, playing some demented, weird game with my mind. Or maybe Timmy really did scare him off. How would I know? It was not knowing that had always driven me absolutely crazy.

Anyway, there was no way I was going into the water after Alex. I couldn't even believe he was there! What did he do, hop in the car for a little six-hour drive to take a dip?

Alex came out and I looked up at the sky as if I were fascinated by the constellations. He put on all his clothes, sopping wet. Then he turned around and said, "Fuck this ocean."

I actually understood that, since I had felt the exact same way that afternoon. I didn't say anything. He was looking at me. "I didn't kill him and I know you think I did!"

"I never said that. That's completely ridiculous."

"You thought I raced him and I didn't, Carly. I didn't!"

"I believe you. Jesus, calm down."

"I can't calm down! We've never even talked about this! Why don't you hate me? I mean, if I raced him to some unreachable buoy, like a ten-year-old, and he died, you should hate me! I hate that you don't!"

I actually had never thought of it that way.

"Why don't you hate me, then?" I shouted back. "I'm the one who said 'fuck you, Timmy, and left and caused it all!"

"You didn't cause a damn thing, Carly. He committed suicide. He killed himself. He told me he was going to, and he did."

I sort of collapsed into the sand at this point. I wanted him to go away.

"He told you...that?"

"Not in so may words, but he was doing coke, driving like a maniac, skiing off cliffs, and when I told him a hundred times to slow down, to get control, to get help, whatever, he'd just smile and say 'I need to go.' He had a death wish. He just swam straight out to sea without stopping once. I swam and swam after him, but he was so goddamn fast. All that coke, all those drinks." I couldn't stand to hear it, but Alex kept going. "He just couldn't bear the world, you know? The best guy on earth and he can't feel connected to the world. He was in pain all the time. What kind of cruelty is that?"

"He told me he'd stopped. The coke. He promised," I said.

"He lied."

I walked up to the car where Alex had a six-pack of beer. I got it out of the car and came back to where he was standing. I fumbled around in my purse and found a cigarette.

"Don't say one damn word," I warned him. He sat down, too, but not too close to me, for which I was eternally grateful.

I just smoked the cigarette with my eyes closed. Then we both lay down next to one another, but not touching. The stars were amazing that night. Finally I said, "He'd want us to let it go."

Alex got up then, really suddenly, and headed back to the car with me trailing behind him.

I thought, "That's what I don't want, I don't want to trail behind him pleading 'Wait up!'"

"Is that what you drove six hours to tell me?" I asked when we were in the car.

"I don't know." He pulled up in front of the house, and I wondered if he were going to turn around and drive right back to Washington. He didn't say anything. I thought that this most likely meant he wanted me to get out. Finally he put his hand on my lap.

"I'm going to go change. I'll be back in an hour. I'll bring some food."

"Where? Where are you going to change?"

"I have a room at the Hedges," he said. Then he kissed me, and I got out of the car. I was about to turn around and say, "Are you sure you're coming back?" But it would have been the little girl saying it, and I had thrown her out in the ocean. She was with Timmy. No, that didn't sound very nice. I'd hidden her. No, I'd comforted her so much she grew up. That was much better.

I ran into the house.

One hour? I threw my clothes all over the room trying to figure out something to wear, scrubbed up the sticky eggs and washed the counter filled with butter and toast crumbs and tossed all the dishes in the dishwasher, put make-up on and took it off, redid my hair ten times and then told myself, "You're acting like a needy child. Remember, you are independent and strong. He'll have to work really hard to have you. Remember that. Ten, ten, ten!" But then I rationalized that even an adult would act this way. Alex had come to see me and not the other way around. But I didn't know what he wanted. I told myself to calm down.

The knock startled me, even though I knew he was coming.

Alex walked in and was hugging me before I could say hello. We didn't say anything. Finally he pulled back, and then he started kissing me and talking at the same time, "I can't believe you...you're so damn stubborn! I kept calling you at home. I've been a jerk, right?" (Shut up and keep kissing me.) "And then yesterday, I found this picture of you..." (Take off my shirt.) "...and I couldn't believe I wasn't with you."

And suddenly I had this sickening feeling that perhaps, since it was late and I'd had this weird day, this was really a dream and not happening at all. Maybe it was just those pills the shrink had given me to help me sleep. Maybe I was hallucinating, and I wasn't in East Hampton, and I wasn't with Alex, but since I was feeling a bit horny, and Alex was looking fantastic in the dream, and I certainly liked everything he was saying, I decided to go with it and relax a little. So I started kissing him back before it all ended, what fool wouldn't? Then, suddenly, I was more awake, and we were on the couch, and he was acting like an actor would in the movies, all smooth with all the right moves, and that's when I got angry and pushed him away.

"You've been playing games with me all year."

He seemed ready for this. "No, I haven't," he said gently.

"You kiss me one day, ignore me the next, introduce me to other women… **instruct me to date other men and get furious when I follow your advice** and then you hand me this friendship crap. I want to know what's going on."

"You didn't know what you wanted, Carly. You seemed to want someone a little more wild and free. You know?" he said, alluding to John.

"*You* don't have ex-spouses or kids. How much freer can you get?" There was silence. "Maybe you don't want to take it all on."

"I've thought about that. I love your kids. I can do this. We can do this, Carly. We can buy another house, we can do anything we want." He paused. "Domestic help is essential." He smiled.

"Damn right." I smiled back. Then I asked him, being vain and curious, "What do you like about me?"

"Your lower lip," he replied.

"Would it seem egotistical if I asked if there were anything else?"

He just smiled. "You know there's so much else." But he didn't start hugging me again, which was annoying.

I stood up. "You know I'm messy and you'll want to change me like everyone else. You want to be with someone neat and pulled together. It's one of your criteria."

"Carly, you don't fit any of my criteria."

"What about your list?" Alex used to carry a list of attributes a woman needed to have.

"I threw it out." He took both my hands suddenly and looked around the room. "He'd be okay with this," Alex said.

Timmy would be very okay with this, I thought. I felt him right there. "I know. He's not our only connection anymore." But he still is one of them, I assured Timmy, in case he was listening.

"Look, I don't know how you're feeling, but I came all the way up here to tell you that I love you and I want to be with you from now on. We've wasted too much time."

"**You** wasted…"

"You got married!"

"You left for California!"

"For med school. I came back and you were fucking married."

"You could have said *something* in the last fifteen years."

"Let's just say we had lousy timing."

I sighed, not ready to give in. "You know I'm getting stronger. I might actually be okay without you."

Alex always knew when I was lying. He scooped me up and carried me upstairs. We stayed up there for A WEEK. I don't know how I ever lived without him.

THE END

3052418

Made in the USA